AF241783

IN THE SHADOWS
of CANYON ROAD

IN THE SHADOWS
of CANYON ROAD

A Novel

STEW MOSBERG

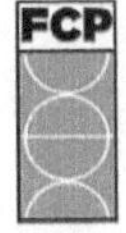

Full Court Press
Englewood Cliffs, New Jersey

Published in the United States of America
by Full Court Press, 601 Palisade Avenue
Englewood Cliffs, NJ 07632
fullcourtpressnj.com

ISBN 978-1-938812-49-1
Library of Congress Control No. 2014960288

*Editing and Book Design by Barry Sheinkopf
for Bookshapers (bookshapers.com)*

Cover Production Art by RubiStarr Designs

Cover Photography and Layout by the author

Colophon by Liz Sedlack

ACKNOWLEDGMENTS

My gratitude goes to all who have encouraged and supported me throughout the undertaking of this book. There are a few among this cherished group of people who deserve special mention. Barry Sheinkopf, my first writing coach, provided the inspiration to fulfill my wordsmithing ambitions. A thank-you to Fred Wildfang for editing and for his kind words on the back cover of this book; and to his wife Diane for reading and enjoying the story. My gratitude also to Sue Lander, McCarson Jones, and Bradley Kachnowicz for their early reading and their heartening reviews, and to Sharon Krinsky for her proofreading and insight, and for being there in the early days.

While this is a work of fiction, I am forever grateful to the many talented artists I know personally and for their passionate desire to create. They remain my greatest inspiration.

—Stew Mosberg,
Bayfield, Colorado
12/2014

PROLOGUE

THE SHADOWS CREEPING ACROSS CANYON ROAD bisect its buildings into chiaroscuro works of art creating blocks of contrasting light and dark that inspired so many artists to move to Santa Fe almost a hundred years ago.

No matter how cold or hot it may be, the clay-colored adobe walls, with their aqua and turquoise trimmed windows and doors, always offer a warm, inviting welcome, like low, sultry flames dancing in a fireplace. Their rounded corners beg to be touched and offer the promise of comfort as if they are old friends.

It is beyond the shadows, behind the walls of the houses and art galleries where the real stories exist.

THE PLAYERS

A Prelude

MARTIN GOMEZ WOKE TO THE CAWING of a raven, rose quietly from the sofa, knocked on the bedroom door to wake his sisters, and called to his brother to get up.

"Hey, R-R-Russ, you better get into the bathroom b-b-before the girls do."

Aunt Téja, her salt and pepper hair tied loosely at the back of her neck, scuffed about in the kitchen brewing coffee and fixing breakfast for the family. The whole house smelled of fried bread and bacon fat.

Kissing her on the top of her head, Martin whispered, "*Buenos*, Tía."

She smiled without looking up. By seven o'clock the youngsters were dressed, fed, and out the door. Téja raced to catch the two buses that would get her to the Wheeler household to start her work day. Martin poured the remaining coffee into a Thermos and walked across the dusty yard to his studio.

The tiny work space was as cold as the early morning air outside, and he blew into his hands and rubbed them together before switching on the small heater; the paint on his palette had frozen during the night; his breath hung in the air for a second and then vanished. Martin squatted in front of the easel and stared at the canvas, deciding what to do next. Mondays were his favorite days—no distractions, only his art, his passion, and precious daylight. He crouched for a long time, studying the colors he had laid down the night before.

Satisfied, he set about chipping the hardened paint from the palette. After futile attempts with a scraper, he resorted to a chisel to pry it loose. When the palette was clean, he squirted new paint onto the board in a clockwise sequence, creating a spectrum of color around the perimeter. He began slowly, stepping back from time-to-time to observe his progress, making tiny grunting noises as he painted, his round face turning this way and that, looking up and down, making sure it all fit the image he held in his mind's eye.

Martin worked for hours unaware of time, until finally, his arms dangling at his sides, a paint rag clutched in one hand and a brush handle held between his teeth, he stopped. It was only then that he felt contented. It was good work, perhaps his best. "*Gracias, Padre,*" he whispered.

He twisted side to side and stretched toward the ceiling, walked to the tiny window, and realized by the shadows it was already time to meet his sisters coming off the school bus.

The following day, far from Martin's studio, Moira Lindstrom was fiddling with the second button on her blouse. She glanced down at her cat. "What do you think, Bruleé. . .too much?"

She adjusted her outfit so only a bit of lacy camisole

showed, gave her brunette hair a once over, ran her tongue across her lips, and reached for the door.

Outside, in the New Mexican morning sunlight, she glanced at the snow-capped Sangre de Cristo Mountains, inhaled the cool, sage-scented air, and slid behind the steering wheel of her white Saab convertible.

The drive to downtown Santa Fe took only a few minutes, and the bells of Saint Francis Basilica began to peal just as she turned off Paseo De Peralta and onto Canyon Road. The sun had already created hard-edged shadows across the quaint adobe buildings, dividing the walls and bright blue doors of the tiny shops and galleries.

She turned onto a side alley, pulled into one of the many hidden courtyards, and parked the car near the back entrance to her restaurant. A painted wooden sign above the door read *Moira Lindstrom's Kiva Café.*

ON A HILLTOP OVERLOOKING the Santa Fe Opera House, Charles Hollingsworth was sitting on his poolside patio, sipping a second cup of coffee. A copy of the Art Newspaper was folded across his legs; at his feet sat a three-year-old gray-and-white bichon frise.

On the Italian marble table, next to the silver creamer and sugar bowl, were stacked copies of *Art News, Southwest Art,* a Christie's Auction catalog, and the *Financial Times.*

Charles, his thick and wavy silver hair neatly combed, was always fastidious about his clothing. At home that morning, he was wearing tennis sneakers, a pair of khaki trousers, and a Ralph Lauren pullover.

His cell phone rang, and Brutus, the little dog, twitched at the intrusion. Hollingsworth reached for the phone, lifted the cover, and waited for the caller to say something.

"Dad?"

"Yes, Vanessa, what is it?"

"Dad, we just uncrated Anise's new painting."

"And?"

"And it's sensational. Her best work ever! I mean it."

"Well, it's about time she pushed the envelope. I was beginning to think she'd run her course."

"Can you come in to see it?"

Charles' jaw tightened and then relaxed. "You know I wasn't planning to be in today. It can wait."

Vanessa drew a deep breath. "Okay. But I want to hang it in the entrance gallery. It will attract a lot of—"

"Wait until I have a look."

He hung up without saying goodbye and flared his nostrils, sensing that Miguel had put too much chlorine in the pool.

AT HOLLINGSWORTH'S GALLEY OF FINE ART, the two assistants held the ends of the large acrylic painting. Vanessa stood amid the scattered wooden slats, excelsior, and bubble wrap, pondering what to do. "Let's just put it in the packing room until Mr. Hollingsworth takes a look."

The young assistants lifted the eight-by-six foot canvas, carefully carried it to the back of the gallery, and gingerly slid it into one of the standing racks.

Vanessa went to her desk, heaved a sigh, bit her lower lip, threw a pencil at the wall, and hissed, "Damn it!"

KEITH WHEELER PLAYED a quick game of Go Fish with his six-year-old daughter Deirdre and then drove her to school before heading to Twin Angels Fine Art. He had started the gallery before his wife Kendra was killed rock climbing in Utah; the child had been only three at the time.

Keith's housekeeper, Téja, helped look after Deirdre and made the house as much of a home as possible. He was not aware that her nephew Martin was an artist, but then almost no one was.

Among the artists exhibited by Twin Angels Gallery was Paolo Rinaldi, a newcomer to the Santa Fe art scene. The young, handsome painter was Keith's discovery. He had seen the artist's work in an obscure European magazine, tracked him down, started a spirited dialog, and offered to represent Paolo in America. He'd introduced Rinaldi to the Canyon Road art community during an opening reception catered by Moira's restaurant. Not long after the event, Keith and Moira's professional arrangement had turned into something more.

THE RINALDI SHOW WAS A RESOUNDING success, and Keith sold eight of the twenty paintings on exhibit that very night, an unbelievable occurrence. With his dark Mediterranean good looks and charming Italian accent, Paolo was a hit with the cognoscenti as well as with the eligible women in town, even a few who were not so eligible.

Rinaldi quickly became Keith's leading seller and the two became friends, albeit on a dealer-client level.

THE LUNCHTIME CROWD had started to build and Moira moved between the kitchen and dining room, checking on meals, the staff, and the patrons. Greeting regulars by their first name or welcoming tourists, she was in her element.

Charles Hollingsworth sauntered in at one o'clock, wearing a pair of beige linen slacks and a blue blazer with a crisp white shirt open at the neck. He sported a pair of tan, tasseled loafers with no socks, and a platinum Tag Heuer watch on his wrist.

Moira noticed him talking with another art dealer and went over to where he was standing.

"Charles! I am surprised to see you here. You usually don't come in on Tuesday."

"Hello, Moira. I have to look at a new painting, but thought I'd have some lunch first."

She lightly touched his hand.

"Let me find you a table. I wish you'd called ahead; we seem to have attracted a lot of out of town people today."

After seating him near the back, but away from the kitchen door, she sauntered off to take care of others waiting at the entrance.

Cydney Rawlings, one of the restaurant's waitresses and sometime assistant manager, leaned on the edge of the bar and placed her order. "Peter. . .table four needs two house reds, a spritzer, and a diet coke."

Peter Portnoy, would-be sculptor and bartender at the restaurant, nodded and called back, "Two merlot, a spritzer, and a diet coke, right. Comin' up."

In addition to the tables Cydney worked, the others were handled by the clandestine artist, Martin "Go-Go" Gomez, whose cutesy moniker was derived from his stuttering.

When asked his name he would stammer, "M-M-Martin

Go-Go-Gomez." Then he'd laugh nervously and offer an apologetic smile.

His shyness was an asset of sorts and made him instantly likable, so no one really teased him. He was also conscientious, fast, and rarely got an order wrong. Little known by any of the employees, including Moira, Martin had studied at a Santa Fe art school and had flourished as a gifted painter until his mother died and he'd had to help support his brother and two younger sisters.

FAR FROM DOWNTOWN SANTA FE, Marta Rodríguez y Encantada rose early, as was her custom. She took tea on the shaded patio with its expansive mountain view and listened to the birds and the splashing water of the fountain.

By most accounts, she was the doyenne of the Santa Fe art community. Her ancestral heritage went back to the conquistadors, and the home she occupied had been built by her family well before the Mexican-American revolution.

According to archival records in the Palace of the Governors, Kit Carson had been a guest in the family's home on a number of occasions, as was General Pershing when he was passing through on the way to battle Pancho Villa.

As patrons of the arts, the Rodríguez y Encantada family frequently provided financial support to help foster cultural activity in New Mexico. The family name graced the doorways of an opera house and several museum collections in the state.

Marta's morning reverie was interrupted by her housekeeper, Lupe. "Doña Marta, I am sorry to disturb you, but you have a phone call."

Marta was scheduled to preside over a ribbon-cutting ceremony commemorating a new addition to the Cultural Center that would house her personal collection of ancient tribal pottery.

The stately lady placed her tea cup on a side table and held out her slender hand to take the phone from the robust woman.

"It is Señor Hollingsworth."

A knowing smile came to the doyenne's lips. "Thank you, Lupe."

Marta straightened her tall, aristocratic frame, and hit the talk button. "Good morning, Charles. How are you?"

"Well, Marta, I am very well. I am looking forward to seeing you Saturday evening and was hoping I might escort you."

Coming from Hollingsworth, it was not an unlikely offer. Anything that could keep him in the spotlight, in the press, particularly the society page, was fair game to him.

"Charles, that is so. . .so, debonair of you." She followed it with a little laugh.

"To the contrary, I would be honored and flattered to be at your side, particularly at such an auspicious occasion. Shall I come by at six?"

"Thank you, Charles, that is quite a compliment, but I have much to do that evening, and I am afraid I would not be very gracious company."

There was a brief silence before he responded.

"Ah. . .well, then, I do understand of course. None-the-less I will seek you out. Oh. . ." he paused and then added, "Congratulations, Marta."

She thanked him, turned the phone off, stretched, and caught the aroma of burning piñon logs from a distant chimney.

She then crossed the patio and headed to the stable, where she kept Callo, her chestnut Morgan, and his stable mate Viento, a magnificent gray Andalucían stallion. Viento had been a gift from a Saudi prince for whom she had helped acquire an art collection.

Marta rode as often as she could, but today she only intended to brush the steeds. When she walked into the barn, her stable man and sometime chauffeur was cleaning the stalls and had already watered and fed both horses.

"Good morning, David. How are you today?"

He straightened up, rested a pitchfork against the side of the stall, ran a hand through his thinning brown hair, and smiled. "I am well today, Doña Marta, and you?"

She smiled. "I am also well."

"Will you be riding this morning?" he asked.

"No. I'm afraid I have too much preparation for the opening. I'll just brush them today."

He nodded, "Certainly. Shall I bring them out?"

"I will take them, thank you."

She spent the next hour grooming the two horses, and then went back to the main house and prepared for the day ahead.

THE CROWD AT THE KIVA had dissipated; the tables had been cleared and set for the dinner hour. Moira sat in her tiny office, going over the menu for Saturday's gala event, which Marta had personally asked her to cater.

BARBARA DEARBORN-HOLLINGSWORTH struggled to get out of bed. It was mid-afternoon; her head throbbed, her mouth was dry, and she had a bitter coating on her tongue; her stomach was queasy, the previous night's binge the second one in a month when she couldn't remember who she had been with or how she got home.

Barbara was Vanessa Hollingsworth's stepmother. She and Charles had finally split when he found her passed out on the living room floor, an empty bottle of Absolut by her side, a pool of vomit under her head.

It had not been the first time he found her in that state, but when she had sobered, if she was ever completely sober, he confronted her, promising it would be the last.

She stared at him like a small child, as if not sure what was being said, and slurred, "Whatta you talking about?"

He turned away, shaking his head. "I've got to get to the gallery. Clean yourself up and think about what I just told you."

A week later she had been out all night, come home at noon, and passed out in the upstairs bedroom. Charles had found her sprawled across the unmade bed, still in her clothes.

At first, he'd experienced a rush of anger, than a stew of emotions—frustration, crushing disappointment, sadness, and total despair. He had called his lawyer that evening and started proceedings.

When they first met, she had been a stunning photographic model—witty, intelligent, and had a decent inheritance from her grandmother—so Charles had felt certain her attraction to him was not his wealth.

Now pushing fifty, Barbara was still attractive to any man who met her, but the drinking had taken a toll and her once sought-after cover-girl face was a little puffy, the circles under her green eyes more difficult to conceal, and her skin dull and fatigued.

For a long time after his first wife Christine died of ovarian cancer, Charles had been a shadow of himself. And Vanessa, still in her teens, had had to deal largely by herself with the emotional turmoil of losing her mother. It was the gumption she'd inherited from her that helped her to survive and ultimately thrive.

When Charles first met Barbara, it'd rejuvenated him and when they married; no one, not even his daughter, had doubted he was madly in love with her. Even after their divorce he probably still was.

Vanessa, closer in age to Barbara than she was to her mother, became friends with Barbara and never felt comfortable calling her a step-mother. They spent a good deal of time together, shopping, having afternoon coffee klatches, going to the movies, and when necessary, which was often, cajoling Charles. When Barbara began sinking deeper into alcoholism, it pained Vanessa greatly; losing another person close to her was more than she was ready to accept. On several occasions, Vanessa tried talking to her about it and finally just blurted it out when they were in Taos for the day. Barbara had started drinking at lunch and by four o'clock had downed four tequila sunrises.

"Barb, you have to stop drinking."

"I'm fine."

"No, actually you're not. You are out of control. You're going to kill yourself. You are going to lose my father. You're going to lose me. You are—"

"I said I'm *fine*," Barbara growled.

Vanessa reached across the table and took her hand, but she tried to pull it away. Vanessa tightened her grip, looked into the other's reddened eyes, and saw they had begun to fill with tears.

"Barbs, I love you, my dad is mad about you, everyone cares about you."

"I *can't*," she all but cried. "I can't stop. I try, but I *can't stop*. I know it is taking me down, but I can't. . . ." She started to shake, and people in the restaurant looked over at them.

Vanessa let go of Barbara's hand and stood up.

"Come on, let's get out of here."

She held on to Barbara's arm to steady her as they walked to the car. It was her hope to have a heart-to-heart on the drive home, but the tequila took its toll and Barbara fell into a stupor as soon as the car started to move.

After that incident, they tried to get Barbara into rehab, but although she said she was willing, it never happened.

In time, Vanessa's compassion turned to pity, and then grew into disrespect and eventually resentment. Within a year, she gradually stopped spending time with Barbara, but always felt enormous guilt not being able to help.

CHAPTER ONE

Seeds Of Discontent

LATE AFTERNOON SHADOWS spread from one side of Canyon Road to the other, and only a few gallery-hopping tourists strolled along the tree-lined street. As often happens in New Mexico when the sun sets, the sky provided a light-show unseen anywhere else. Hues of purple, orange, and pink melded into one another, turning the sky magenta and then blood red, until it morphed into a deep indigo and disappeared.

In the hour leading up to the atmospheric phenomenon, tourists clamor for balcony seats at restaurants and bars, where they can witness the magical occurrence.

Moira inspected the dining room and checked on the kitchen staff before heading over to the Twin Angels Gallery. Stopping at the doorway to Keith's office, she playfully called out, "Knock, knock."

He looked up from the monitor just as she dropped into a chair and kicked off her shoes. "Mind if I sit for a few minutes? My feet are killing me. That is, if you're not too busy."

He shook his head. "What's up?"

"It's been non-stop, Keith. The kitchen's buzzing twelve hours a day, and we're prepping for Saturday's reception. You're coming, right?"

"Yes, of course."

"Oh, goody, I miss you. How's it going over here?"

"Busy, but trying to be home when Deirdre gets back from school."

"How is that little sweet pea of yours?

Keith smiled, his eyes instinctively seeking the framed photo of his daughter.

"Gonna look just like her mom."

The sadness that used to fill his eyes when he spoke of Kendra had gradually faded with time, replaced by warm memories.

"I wish I'd known her."

"Kendra? Yeah, you two would've gotten along great."

"So tell me," she asked.

"Tell you what?"

"What've you been up to?"

"Like I said—"

She waved her hand. "I know, same ol', same ol'. But really, Keith, what's going on?

He squinted. "Why do I have the feeling you're searching for something more definitive?"

She threw her head back and laughed, low and throaty, almost sexy, but not quite. While she waited for a response, she surveyed the interior of his work space. The walls were filled with photos, more than a few of Deirdre, two of Kendra, one in which she was hanging by one hand, free-climbing a butte in Moab.

Behind the desk were three crayon drawings by his daughter, a credenza lined with art books, a few Mata Ortiz pottery pieces, and a black-and-white photograph of Leo Castelli, the New York art dealer, his arm on the shoulder of a very young Keith Wheeler.

She turned her attention back to Keith. "Okay," she pouted, "then don't tell me."

"Come on, Moira, what's on your mind?"

She clasped her long fingers and placed her hands on the edge of the desk.

"How are you and Rinaldi working out?"

He was surprised by the inquiry. "Where'd that come from?"

"My dear Mr. Wheeler," she started, "I may not be the brightest color on your palette, but I know when one dealer's artist is being courted by another."

Growing impatient with the cat and mouse game, he exhaled. "And your point is?"

"Hollingsworth was in for lunch yesterday. He ate alone, lingered over an espresso, and then was joined by your Italian Stallion."

Keith sat straight up, arched his back, and pensively brought a finger to his lips. "So?"

"That's it? That's all you have to say?"

"Moira, it's a small world—the art world. . .especially Canyon Road. We all know each other. Might just've been a chance meeting."

"Umm, are you being naive, or just stubborn?"

"Moira, do you *know* something, or is this supposition on your part?"

"I don't know for *sure*, I couldn't exactly eavesdrop. But—"

"Do you really think they'd be in collusion in broad daylight, knowing it would probably get back to me? Besides, what do you think is going on? Paolo and I are tight. I give him a very fair deal and a lot of wall space."

Still concerned over what she thought might be an indiscretion, she pressed on. "I'm sure that's true, but I'm also not the best person to determine that. I just know what I saw. And they seemed awfully chummy."

He took a deep breath and ran his fingers through his blond, Redfordesque hair.

"Thanks, Moira. I appreciate your telling me. I'll think about it, okay?"

She looked directly into his penetrating blue eyes, placed her hands on his, and looked at them; they were strong hands, calloused slightly at the fingertips, nails uneven but clean.

They said nothing for a few moments before she stood up, "Okay, just wanted you to know, that's all. Do with it what you want."

She walked to the door, turned around, came back, and kissed him. "Look forward to seeing you Saturday. Have a great rest of the day."

"You, too."

He followed her with his eyes, her slim body silhouetted in the doorway, the late afternoon sun highlighting her hair with touches of red, the faint outline of her legs teasingly visible through the fabric of her skirt. Smiling, he briefly pictured her naked, then shook the image out of his mind and turned back to the computer.

CHARLES SWAGGERED INTO his gallery around three o'clock and found Vanessa and the gallery assistants moving some artwork.

There was a large blank space on the far wall directly opposite the front window. She turned her attention to the door when her father walked in.

Without so much as hello, Charles launched into a declaration. "I decided to get things in order before the no-taste tourists get here."

Vanessa was wearing a beige linen skirt, a pair of braided leather sandals, toes painted a subtle pink; her blouse, a white Mexican peasant chemise, was cinched at the waist with a bright pink sash, her hair pulled back in a neat pony tail.

She managed a cheery, "Hi, Dad."

"Making room for the new Anise?"

"Yes, we are." She beseechingly took his hand. "Come let me show it to you; it's in the store room."

Charles folded his arms. "Bring it out here so I can look at it in the light. Then I'll decide where it should go."

Vanessa sighed, having already cleared wall space for it.

"Madeleine…Dennis," she called, "bring the Anise out, so Mr. Hollingsworth can have a look."

The two young people brought the work into the main gallery and stood on each side of it, holding it aloft.

Charles moved from side to side, trying to avoid reflected light from the window behind him. He stood with his hand cupping his chin, squinting, coming in close and then stepping back a few feet. The room was silent, except for the hum of a computer hard drive. Vanessa held her breath and audibly exhaled when she saw the corners of Charles' mouth turn up and he started nodding.

"Well, you're right, it is a great work. . .definitely her best in. . .I love that heavy impasto she's—and the juxtaposition of color is. . .I like this composition. As a non-representational canvas, this has elements I haven't seen before. . .very dynamic. . .lots of. . . ." He stepped closer. "Is that paper mixed in with the paint?"

"Yes, she's bonded euros to it, and up at the top she's pasted stock quotes from the European bourse."

"What'd she title it?"

"Worldly Goods-Global Chaos."

A wry smile crossed Charles' face, and it was clear that he not only approved, but agreed with his daughter. Vanessa was beaming.

She motioned with her chin. "Don't you think it should hang on that wall?"

"Go ahead and give it a try, but make sure there's no glare on it. I'll be in my office."

Vanessa felt much better. The two assistants were dressed in similar black slacks and sweaters; they showed no emotion but stood waiting for a sign from Vanessa to proceed. She took a step backward, tilted her head to one side, and then moved to the entrance doorway and shook her head.

"Hoist away!"

The hanging hooks had already been positioned; the two

assistants stood on stepladders on either side of the painting and gingerly raised it as they moved up one step at a time; the painting went up in minutes. When it was in place, the three of them stood together.

"Love it!" cried Dennis, his hands clasped in front of him.

Dennis, tall and willowy like Madeleine, looked like her twin. She purposely bumped him with her hip.

"Dennis, you love everything! How is anyone supposed to know what is good art, and what is crap, when you're the critic?"

He returned the hip bump and walked to the desk they shared at the back of the gallery.

CHAPTER TWO

Change In The Wind

Doña Marta pulled up on the reins and brought Callo to a halt a few yards from the stable entrance. The horse was lathered from a hard ride; beads of moisture had formed above Marta's lip and behind her ears; her blouse was wet at the small of her back. Dave hurried over and assisted her off the horse.

Exhilarated, she brushed stray hairs from her eyes, took a deep breath, exhaled, and patted the horse's flank. "Good ride, *caballo*, good ride."

She ducked under the horse's head and handed the reins to the stable man.

"Please walk him until he cools down, and groom him carefully, David."

"Yes of course, as you wish, Doña Marta."

She was happy: the morning was splendid, the air deliciously scented and cool, and she felt completely prepared for the upcoming gala. Minutes after the dry cleaner delivered her outfit, a floral arrangement arrived from Charles Hollingsworth. It contained a note congratulating her and wishing her well—

a typically obsequious gesture from the man, but Marta appreciated the sentiment all the same; she loved fresh-cut flowers. The day had started well, and the gallery unveiling promised to be even better.

Martin returned to his family's modular house well after ten in the evening. He kissed his aunt, looked in on his sleeping sisters and then on his brother Russell, who was still doing homework.

"Hey, little brother, how'r you d-d-doing?"

"Hey, Martin, how goes it?"

"What are you w-working on?"

"I am doing a book report for English. But *a-i-i-i Dio*, it is not my thing."

Martin laughed. "I know," he said, "Eng-glish is not my th-thing either."

They laughed together, and then Martin let his younger brother go back to his studies. Téja was watching television but looked up when he came into the room.

"Do you want something to eat, *joven*?"

"No, *Tía*, I'm good. I want to do some work. I will see you in the morning."

Téja nodded and went back to the shopping network jewelry show. She never bought anything from it but liked to look at the dazzling array of goods that others ordered readily.

"Where do they get the money?" she wondered aloud. "How many arms and fingers do they have, to wear it all?"

She herself had only one piece of jewelry, a rosary that had belonged to her grandmother. It was made of pure silver and had been blessed by the cardinal in Albuquerque more than a hundred years before. Other than her family, she cherished it more than anything else.

Martin painted in a dilapidated garage behind his house. The roof was in need of repair, but he patched it and sealed the walls as best he could to keep the cold and snow from getting in. For the most part it was airtight, if not exactly warm.

He took a few minutes to adjust to the light, switched on the generator, blew into his hands, and then walked around, studying the newly completed work.

On the canvas, he had blended soft blue, light purple, and pale greens; the scumbled background morphed into ghost-like figures in the foreground. The theme, *Spirits in a Mist*, he would call it, was otherworldly, dreamlike, and set in an old cemetery. Three black crosses atop a chapel rooftop vanished into the background.

Martin crossed over to a recently finished work leaning against the wall; the painting was completely different. He had originally sketched the scene in the fall while hiking in the mountains near Angel Fire. The leaves, based on mental notes he had made, were dazzling yellow, orange, auburn, and russet set against a stark, pure cerulean blue sky, with a single wispy cloud.

Near the lower section of the canvas was a stream bordered by the narrow trunks of several white-and-black mottled aspen trees, and in the foreground, some bright red chokeberries.

Martin bent over an old taboret he had scrounged from a junk heap long before; on it were some used yellow-and-red Café Bustelo coffee cans filled with wood-handled paint brushes. Most of the bristles were worn down to rounded, uneven hackles from what had once been square tips. And although well used, they were his proud possessions and lovingly maintained as best as he could. The air in the room was a heady mixture of turpentine and mineral spirits, linseed oil, and dammar varnish.

Martin stood there for several minutes considering his efforts, then sighed and lifted a blank canvas onto one of the easels. Preparing a painting surface was another source of pride for him.

He loved the process and the sense of accomplishment he derived when they were completed: taut and straight, the corners neat and flat, all mounted to pre-treated wood that was solid and would not warp.

It was more time consuming to build them in such a traditional manner, but he was particular.

He went about adding fresh pigment to his palette, mixed some colors, pushed a one-inch wide brush into the blend, and then raised it to the top of the canvas and pressed the bristles against the surface, vigorously moving the brush back and forth, scumbling several colors into an amorphous background.

Martin worked until it became so uncomfortably cold that his vaporous breath co-mingled with his vision of the work-in-progress. He stopped, cleaned his brushes, turned off the generator, and hurried back to the house.

Téja had fallen asleep on the sofa; the light from the television bathed the room in a flickering eerie blue. He covered her with a woven blanket, turned off the TV, and looked in on his siblings. The house was quiet. His brother was sound asleep; a book lay on the floor next to his cot; the lamp was still lit.

The girls usually slept in bunk beds but were curled up together in the lower one. Martin smiled, knowing they were okay and reasonably warm.

His aunt stirred, opened her eyes, and tried to focus. She reached for the glasses dangling from the chain around her neck, placed them on the bridge of her nose without putting them on her ears, and squinted at Martin.

"Oh, I am sorry, *joven*, I didn't mean to fall asleep on your bed."

"S'okay, Tía. Go b-b-back to sleep."

She rose anyway, gave him a kiss on the cheek, walked sleepily to the girls' room, and lay down on the single bed. Martin pulled a sheet from under the sofa cushions, tucked it in, and leaned one of the pillows against the arm rest. He undressed in the dark, got under the blanket, and quickly fell asleep.

IN SPITE OF ALL THERE WAS TO DO, Marta lingered over a cup of chai tea, read the newspaper, and perused the arts and leisure section, taking particular note of the entry about the evening's ceremonies.

When she was finished, she moved to the study and brought another cup of tea with her. The room included a floor-to-ceiling bookcase running the length of the wall; an enormous oriental rug filled the wooden floor to within two feet of the walls. Facing the French doors leading to the patio stood a large antique desk that had belonged to her great-grandfather.

On it, she kept his silver-and-glass ink-well and leather-trimmed blotter, and a photo of her family at an Easter reunion taken years earlier.

She also had a laptop on the desk but rarely used it, preferring to do her business in person, on hand-written note cards, or through telephone calls.

On the side opposite the bookcase, there were two easy chairs and an overstuffed couch with brightly colored pillows; a cocktail table was adorned with small Zuni pottery and thick illustrated books on the work of Diego Rivera, Frida Khalo, and Jose Clemente-Orozco. On the far wall, opposite her desk, hung an original El Greco.

She skimmed through a few documents, checked her note pad and address book, and made calls to people involved with the special evening, including the entertainers—a mariachi band and a Native American drummer, singer, and dancer.

Following her calls, she outlined what she wanted to say and listed the names of those she wished to publicly thank. Her handwriting reflected her personality, elegant and refined.

She was finished by lunchtime and asked Lupe to make her a small salad and a glass of papaya juice, and bring it to her on the patio.

By four p.m., Marta had taken a short nap and bathed, and by five was dressed in a black tunic top with gray flannel slacks, simple and stylish, as was her preference.

David drove her to the Cultural Center in the Jaguar, saw her up the steps, and said he would return at nine p.m.

CHAPTER THREE

The Cultured

KEITH RACED HOME FROM THE GALLERY after a last-minute customer came in wanting to see some gicleé prints. The man deliberated for half an hour and finally said he would talk it over with his wife and be back the next day.

Deirdre was having dinner when Keith got home; Téja was sitting at the table with her eating a *chalupa*.

The youngster screeched, "Daddy!" jumped up from her Spaghetti-O's, her personal favorite, and rushed to him.

He hoisted her up, gave her a purposely sloppy kiss, and put her down.

"Yuk!" she exclaimed, dragging her open hand across her face.

"Is that what you think of Daddy's kisses?" he teased.

She shrugged and shoved a spoonful of the little orange vowels into her mouth.

"Sorry I can't join you in such gourmet fare, Dimples, but I have to change my clothes and get to the Center; I'm running late."

"It's okay, Daddy, Tay-ha is going to watch *Frozen* with me."

"Didn't you just watch that last week?"

"Yes, and I watched it the week before that. But Olaf is sooo-oo cute!"

Keith looked at Téja and rolled his eyes. The woman smiled. "It is very good with me, Mr. Keith. I like to hear this little one laugh. It makes me laugh, too."

Feeling satisfied Deirdre was okay with his not being there to tuck her in, he went upstairs, quickly showered and dressed, and arrived at the Center to find the mayor's opening salutation almost completed. He remained at the back of the room and listened.

". . .It is a testament to the unwavering generosity of the Rodríguez-Encantada family, and in particular, our beloved Doña Marta."

Marta stood off to the side of the podium; opposite her was the Director of the Cultural Center, Mildred Hathaway, Ph.D. The mayor concluded his remarks and handed the microphone to Hathaway.

The director, in her early fifties, short and stocky but not obese, cleared her throat, slid her glasses onto her nose, glanced at Marta, and then turned to the assembly. "It is with great pride and a sense of enormous gratitude that I am here to honor the city of Santa Fe with a collection of extraordinary value, both historically and artistically. None of this would be possible without the tireless efforts of Doña Marta Rodríguez-Encantada. Not only has she made munificent contributions to the arts, for which her family is so well known, but officially, as of this very special evening, she has donated her personal collection of historic Anasazi artifacts to our Cultural Center. In so doing, it is only fitting, and yet a small token of our appreciation, to name the place that will house these magnificent objects. . .the Rodríguez-Encantada Gallery."

Applause filled the room. Hathaway stepped back from the podium, reached for Marta's hand, kissed her on both cheeks, and thanked her for the people of Santa Fe.

The doyenne's bearing was aristocratic, her smile luminous. She waited a moment, clasped her hands on the podium, and did not refer to her notes.

"I will keep my words brief, but would like to thank all of you who have contributed your time and effort, and your financial backing, and for your love of the arts and the ancients. Tonight, we share in the joy and sense of accomplishment this gallery represents, and I am most grateful for your support. It is my sincere wish that the collection behind this ribbon will help portray our forbears, the first people, as the artisans—the sensitive and unique people that they were—and that this gallery will bring us all closer together in spirit and understanding."

The mayor approached with large brass scissors, and the two of them, photographers snapping pictures, cut the ribbon. He then linked arms with Marta and stepped into the gallery, while the mariachis began to play and the crowd moved forward.

The mood was festive with pockets of laughter and a good deal of mingling among the guests, setting the tone for an evening of conviviality.

The collection was exceptionally well lit and attractively displayed; the pottery—some tiny, others the size of watermelons—could be easily studied from many vantage points.

Photographs of ancient Anasazi dwellings hung from the ceiling, along with enlarged 19th-century Edward Curtis photo reproductions of tribal elders. At seven p.m. the ancestral drum thumped, and Native music filled the gallery with a spiritual chanting. When the Zuni elder finished blessing the gallery, he and his companions left the room.

Keith lingered at the back until a lilting voice redirected his attention. "Well, there you are."

He turned to face Moira.

"Enjoying yourself?" she asked.

"Absolutely! Can I get you a drink?"

"That would be lovely. I'll come with you."

As they made their way to the bar, she took his hand, gave a gentle squeeze, and then let go. A voice from behind them called out, "Keith! Moira!"

It was Bill Yarbrough, owner of Gallery 212.

They responded in unison, "Hello, Bill."

Yarbrough, in a maroon velvet jacket, white shirt, and tan pants, smiled broadly, first at Keith and then Moira before offering a greeting: "Lovely night, isn't it?"

"Yes, it really is," said Keith. "Good to see you, Bill."

Bill tilted his glass towards the two of them and said, "Well. . .enjoy." He lightly touched Keith's arm and brushed by.

Keith ordered the wine and looked around at the gathering. "Nice turn-out."

"Yes. . .we were expecting around eighty. Looks like we're pretty close to that."

Marta, a few steps beyond them and surrounded by several men and two women, glanced at Moira and Keith, gestured for them to wait, and then left the group and walked over.

"Moira, thank you for all your wonderful work—everything is delicious and beautifully presented. I knew you would be the right choice for this evening. . .and, Keith, how nice to see you. Thank you for coming. How is your darling daughter—Deirdre, isn't it?"

She offered her hand, and he took it in his and smiled at the acknowledgment. "I am thrilled to be here," he said, "and to see the collection in its entirety. You are a gift to our community. As for Deirdre—thank you for remembering; she is a delight, as always."

"She really is an adorable child, and so well-mannered. You have done a splendid job. Now, please forgive me, but I must share myself with many people tonight. It is good to see you both."

As she walked away, Keith focused his attention beyond her. Moira turned to see what he was looking at and spotted Charles Hollingsworth against the far wall, drink in hand, talking animatedly to. . .Paolo Rinaldi.

CHAPTER FOUR

Conspiracy

HOLLINGSWORTH LAUGHED PATRONIZINGLY at something Paolo said, then placed his arm on the Italian's shoulder, leaned in, and whispered in his ear. A few more words were exchanged between them before they shook hands and went in different directions.

"Not too discreet, are they?" asked Moira.

Keith had a quizzical look on his face; the glass of wine in his hand remained poised mid-air, his mouth open in disbelief.

"So now what do you think?" she asked.

It was a few seconds before Keith took a sip of the wine and then downed the rest. He scratched his forehead and watched Rinaldi walk toward a group of people and sidle up to a tall, attractive woman, Barbara Dearborn-Hollingsworth.

"Maybe you were right," Keith muttered. "I'm not sure what to make of it, but I'll—"

"Keith. . .Hollingsworth can't be trusted. You have to *say* something."

"To whom, Charles? Paolo? I don't want to get into a bidding war. If Rinaldi is unhappy, then he'll leave no matter what."

She rested a hand on his arm and stepped closer so no one would hear, "Keith, sweetie, you have to act quickly. If Charles is trying to lure him away from your gallery, assuming he hasn't already, you need to cut it off now."

"Like I said, I'm not into bidding wars. Painters come and painters go, just as galleries do. I am not so arrogant as to think—"

"To think what?"

"Moira, life is not all that scripted, if he leaves, well …" he paused and then added, "I've lost more than that in my life."

She pressed her lips together to stifle a comment.

Keith held her gaze. "Thank you. I appreciate your concern. I really do."

It was apparent that he didn't want to continue the topic, so she ended by saying, "If you want to talk about it, you know where to find me."

He looked at his watch. "There's still time to have another drink."

Before she could reply, there was a shattering of glassware, followed by a stunned silence. Heads turned toward the commotion. It was embarrassingly easy to hear Charles Hollingsworth from every corner of the gallery. "C'mon, Barbara, you've had enough."

She violently pulled her arm away from his grasp. "Get away from me. You're not. . . ."

She swayed a tiny bit, but Charles caught her by the elbow and herded her toward the exit, where she became bellicose.

"Who the fuck 'r *you* to—"

He ushered her outside as the broken glass was quickly swept up. A few of the guests murmured and shook their heads; others shrugged as though it were a normal occurrence.

Marta motioned to the mariachis, and they instantly broke into song.

Keith raised his eyebrows, smirked, and then turned toward Moira. "Well?"

"I'd love to go somewhere else with you right now, but I'm working and can't leave until everything is cleared out."

"I'm sorry—I forgot this was your shindig."

He took hold of her hand, brought it to his lips, kissed it, and then leaned in and brushed her lips ever so lightly with his own.

"Good night, sugar," he whispered.

"Sweet dreams, Keith."

He turned, scanned the room for Paolo, and spotted him with four people—a married couple he knew as major donors to the Santa Fe Ballet, and two ceramicists; he walked over.

"*Buona sera, Paolo. Como se va?*"

Paolo turned his head at the sound of the voice, his dark Mediterranean eyes registering only a hint of concern; he raised his glass of wine toward Keith and replied, "*Ah, buona sera, padrone mio.*"

"Can I speak with you a moment, Paolo?"

The artist made a gesture of contrition to his companions, murmured, "*Scuze,*" and then stepped away.

Keith nudged him out of the group's earshot and flat-out asked, "Tell me, my friend, do we have a problem?"

Paolo's face contorted. "What do you say?"

Keith was not in the mood. "Paolo, I know you've been talking to Hollingsworth."

The painter responded without emotion, "And why is that a *problem?*"

For a moment, Keith wondered if he was right. What, indeed, did it have to do with anything? Certainly, Canyon Road was a small art community. Everyone knew everyone who worked there or was represented on the street.

Keith hesitated, thought of what Moira had said, and then reconsidered that perhaps the whole thing was nothing of significance.

Paolo smiled a bright toothy, boyish grin and cocked his head. "My art," he joked, "is in your hands. No problem. You are my *padrone.*"

Still uncertain, Keith asked, "Yes, Paolo, but for how long? Has Charles made an offer to you? Is he trying to lure you away from The Twin Angels Gallery?"

Rinaldi fidgeted.

Keith waited for a response and began to feel anxious, but held his ground. Paolo looked across the room as if seeking someone to rescue him.

"Well? Is he?" demanded Keith.

Rinaldi, like a child caught in a lie, shrugged.

"He is, isn't he? That son of a bitch! How dare he? And right under my nose. The man has no scruples."

Rinaldi shifted his weight and looked down at his expensive shoes. He tugged at the white silk scarf around his neck and began fingering its knotted fringe.

"Paolo, I'll be in the gallery tomorrow. You can come by at any time to talk about this, or if you need time to get your priorities straight, come in on Tuesday."

The artist, visibly uncomfortable, hesitated, "Uhh. . . ."

Keith's expression was grim, but he didn't want to show how annoyed he was by the ambivalence, particularly in public. Before walking away, he lowered his voice and said, "Until Tuesday, Paolo."

By the time he pulled into the garage, Téja and Deirdre were asleep. Still upset, he went to the fridge and grabbed a long-neck bottle of Tecate. He sat in the darkened living room, mulling over the night's events, not the least of which was Moira and his growing affection for her.

The more pressing concern, however, at least at the moment, was Paolo. Losing Rinaldi as one of his artists would be a financial blow, but to lose him to Hollingsworth was insulting. He tugged at the beer and pondered his moves. Painters come and painters go, just as galleries do; wasn't that what he had said to Moira? He brought the bottle to his mouth, swallowed the last of the brew, and went to bed.

THE POOLSIDE TABLE WAS SET with brightly colored linens and Ettore Sottsass-designed coffee serving pieces. Charles brewed a pot of Lavazza dark roast and took it out to the patio; playing softly on the sound system was a concerto by Albinoni. He was dressed for work, wearing a linen blazer and a pale blue shirt and gray slacks, and was already well into the auction section of the Art Newspaper when the door chimes rang.

Fiona, the housekeeper, just back from morning services

at Loretto Chapel, went to the door and led the guest through the house to the patio. Hollingsworth stood up.

"Ah, Paolo, you look no less the worse for wear after last night's festivities." Then, in a gesture of regret, he lowered his voice and added, "I'm sorry about the embarrassing incident with my former wife, but. . . ."

Rinaldi was wearing neatly pressed designer jeans, a pale yellow sport shirt, and no jacket. His black hair still wet from a shower, was combed straight back, revealing his strong features and intense brown eyes.

He raised a hand, palm up. "*Basta, Padrone,* no need to say anything."

Hollingsworth pulled a chair away from the table, "Please sit down. Coffee?"

The painter looked around the property: the pool, the view of mountains in the distance, the furnishings and accessories. He quickly studied the composition, the light, and the lifestyle of his host.

"You have a very lovely villa, *Signore* Hollingsworth."

Charles smiled politely. "Please call me Charles."

Paolo tilted his head in deference. "Charles."

Fiona brought a tray of scones, croissants, jam, and butter, placed them on the table, and left without a word. Hollingsworth poured coffee for his guest and offered the basket of baked goods. The Genoan took a croissant and slowly buttered it without taking his eyes off Charles.

"Let me get right to the point," suggested Hollingsworth. "You are a great painter. Your work is excellent and is already developing a reputation as a solid investment. It is wonderful that Twin Angels brought you here, but Keith Wheeler lacks. . . how shall I say it? The book—"

Rinaldi, clearly not certain of the reference, furrowed his brow.

"Sorry. By 'book,' I mean a following of clients that can pay higher prices—people who will collect your work, who can afford to pay for private commissions. Wheeler doesn't have the. . .connections I have. I can get you exhibitions in museums and press coverage in magazines that count, not only the local variety."

Paolo nodded and brought the pastry to his mouth, paused, and sniffed the warm, fresh scent, the zesty Valencia orange marmalade, and the rich butter, took a tiny bite, and placed it back on his plate.

Hollingsworth watched Rinaldi's handsome face for a flicker of recognition, of some interest, a sign that he was listening, and more importantly, to see if he seemed to be considering the proposition.

A breeze wafted across the pool, rippling the water. Paolo moved his head slightly in time to the music, took a sip of coffee, and remained silent.

The gallery owner leaned forward and placed his elbows on the table. "Paolo, I have just offered you an opportunity. Do you understand what I have said?"

The painter peered into his host's eye, looked away momentarily and then back again. He took a breath before speaking, carefully forming the words in his adopted language. "My dear friend, you only suggest an opportunity to me. But you have not made an offer."

Charles considered whether he had underestimated the Italian's business acumen. "You are right, Paolo, but before I provide details, I must know your interest, your intentions. Quite frankly, you haven't told me if you're willing to leave the Twin Angels Gallery."

Paolo sat back in the chair but remained silent.

Hollingsworth's patience was beginning to thin. He looked at his watch. Brutus suddenly leapt up from under the table, began yelping at a squirrel crossing the patio, and took off after it.

Rinaldi followed the chase with his eyes, laughed, and turned back to Charles. "He is fast, no? But not fast enough to catch the prey."

Charles didn't miss the painter's innuendo. He cleared his throat and tried again to elicit a response from his guest. "Paolo let me be more specific. The most Twin Angels has gotten for a painting of yours is what—twenty-eight five? Am I right?"

Rinaldi raised an eyebrow.

Charles got into it. "I am aware of what sells on Canyon Road and what was paid for it. Be assured, my young friend, there is nothing that gets past me here. But I can promise you this: You join Hollingsworth Gallery, and in two years they will be demanding *twice* that amount."

Rinaldi nodded, scratched at his chin.

"*Que dici?* You. . .uh. . .say a big number, yes?"

"Yes. But not something I can't deliver. *Now* are you interested?"

Rinaldi grinned. "That is what I come to hear, so now you

say more."

Charles had hoped to be less explicit.

"Tell me, Paolo, what would it take to bring you into my gallery? What do you want out of life?"

Rinaldi softened a bit; the cleft in his angular chin seemed to deepen as he flashed a brilliant smile.

"I think to be the best painter since Caravaggio. I would paint what *I* want to paint, not what anyone else wants me to paint. I would enjoy life and live to be one hundred. I want to travel and—"

Charles waved him off. "Yes, yes, my friend. You can have all that and more."

"So how will this be?"

"As far as I know, you have no written agreement with Keith Wheeler. Correct?"

"No. We just shake hands. I trust him."

"I understand, but art is a business, and in business a handshake is difficult to hold on to."

Paolo peered into the coffee cup as if he were studying it for composition.

CHARLES, GIVING HIM TIME TO THINK, lifted the Art Newspaper and perused the front page headline: *Sotheby's, Christie's Sales Beat Last Year's, Chinese Contemporary Art Sales Shows Signs of Slowing*. He had started to turn the page when Paolo cleared his throat and stood up.

Charles folded the paper and put it on the table.

"Yes, I think," the Italian began, "art is a business, but I am a painter and business is more easy for businessmen, no?"

"Meaning what exactly?"

"Meaning that I must think more about what you have said."

"Take your time, my friend, but speak to no one of this."

Charles rose and put his hand on Rinaldi's shoulder to lead him out. He stopped at the doorway, took a tiny engraved card from a side table, and handed it to him.

"Here is my private number. Call me when you have made a decision."

They shook hands and Charles reached for the door, said, "*Ciao!*" and let him out.

CHAPTER FIVE

Before the Storm

MANY PEOPLE WHO WORKED FOR or owned a business on Canyon Road took Mondays off. Moira slept a bit longer and lingered over coffee and a raspberry scone while CNN droned in the background. Pulling on an old but sleek pair of blue jeans and an oversize sweat shirt, she impulsively decided to drive up to Abiquiu and the Ghost Ranch, where a week-long workshop for *plein air* painters was underway.

The cliffs ringing the ranch were striated with red, amber, and ocher soil and rock formations; leaves of the aspen trees shimmered like golden sequins glittering in the sunlight. Beyond the property's cluster of cabins, small groups of artists, half hidden by easels, were trying to capture the view of the countryside before the light shifted.

Moira meandered from one to the other, moving close enough to look at each painting without being a nuisance. Afterward, she wandered into the foothills, hiked up a rock-strewn rise, and sat on a ridge where she could survey the surrounding landscape. In the quiet of the day, secluded and remote from the Kiva Café, her thoughts drifted to Keith, and a tiny smile came to her lips. She lay back and luxuriated in the afternoon sun and the deliciousness of the moment, while an image of her, Keith, and Deirdre formed in her mind, the three of them hiking up to the same spot on which she lay. Deirdre ran ahead, turning to look at her father and Moira holding hands, and shouted, "Come on, you guys, catch *up!*"

A raven squawked loudly, cutting into her reverie. She blinked, and the image vanished, but the feeling lingered, and at that moment she knew she was falling in love with Keith Wheeler.

She sat up, took a long drink from her water bottle, and headed down the hill. Returning to her car, she lowered the convertible top and headed home, stopping at a bodega along the highway for a coffee and sweet *sopapilla*. Momentarily carefree, cruising down the road, she invited the wind to ravage her hair.

BY LATE TUESDAY AFTERNOON the Twin Angels Gallery had only two walk-ins, and Keith still hadn't heard from Paolo. He had resigned himself to losing the artist and was already considering who he could get to replace him.

Sifting through paperwork, winding down his day, he bolted when the phone rang.

"Twin Angels Gal—"

"I am late calling you," said Paolo. "I know. But—"

"Are you coming in?"

Paolo cleared his throat.

"*Per favore, Padrone,* I must have another day. *Domani* is okay?"

Keith began fiddling with Kendra's climbing clip, swinging it around on his finger like a set of keys. He pondered whether he wanted to do it.

"*Signori?*" inquired Paolo.

Keith inhaled through his nostrils and slowly let the air escape. "Until tomorrow. But if you're not here by ten, we are *finito. Capisce?*"

It was a harsh delivery, but it made a strong statement, and there was no going back for either of them. Keith hung up without saying another word.

Paolo, who had been smiling only moments before, was momentarily crestfallen. He sat on the leather sofa in his studio, scratched his bare chest, and then ran his hand through his hair. "*Dio, mio,*" he muttered.

He reached for a bottle on the paint-spattered coffee table, and filled a glass with a rich Volpolicella and swirled the wine under his nose, allowing it to waft upward into his nostrils.

Heady, but not overpowering; it was a favorite, but under the circumstances, a quick slug of grappa would have been preferable. The door to the bathroom opened, and a willowy blond sauntered into the studio, tucking her blouse into the top of brown suede slacks.

Paolo looked up and smiled, put the glass down, and ambled toward her. She put one arm around his neck and, with the other, squeezed his buttocks. He gently pulled her hair, tilted her head back, and pressed his mouth to hers.

They kissed hotly, his hands running down her back and over the curve of her hips.

"My dear, sweet lady, you are a very beautiful and very, sexy woman."

"And you are a gifted artist. . .in more ways than one. No wonder my ex-hubby wants you."

Paolo traced the contour of her back with both hands, than brought them around and cupped her breasts, squeezing her nipples between his fingers as hard as he dared. She gave a tiny groan and started to kiss his chest, but he pulled his hands away and took a step back. "*Ai*, we must stop now. I have to work. . .and you must go."

"*Why* do I have to go? Can't I stay here?"

"Barbara, I told you, that is not possible. I must paint.   I cannot do that with you or anyone around me."

She pouted, went to the table, and swallowed the rest of Paolo's wine, then poured another glass. "Don't you have any-thing besides this Italian piss water?"

He grimaced and shook his head. "Please. We had a very nice afternoon, no? We can see each other again soon."

"When?"

"Soon." He shrugged. "I don't know when. Soon."

She raised the glass and was about to throw its contents at her lover, but then thought about it and drank it in one gulp, wiping her mouth with the back of her hand.

"You'll miss me when you're finished working. But I won't be here, will I? . . . And when are you going to paint me? You said you wanted to. Isn't that how you got me to come up here that first time?"

Paolo sighed, grabbed the cashmere V-neck hanging on the back of a chair, and slipped it over his head.

"*Ciao, bella.* I will call you tomorrow, yes?"

Barbara shook her head, smiled sardonically, and patted his cheek. "If you weren't so fucking hot, I'd tear your heart out."

"*Ah, cara mia,* you already have."

CHAPTER SIX

A Deal Is A Deal

GOOD MORNING, ANISE. It's Charles. How's my best painter?" Hollingsworth made it a point to sound positively cheerful.

"Hello, Charles. What a lovely surprise, the master dealer calling li'l ol' me? To what do I owe this . . . it *will* be a pleasure, right?"

Charles chuckled. "Anise, let me get right to the point. . . "

"You always do, Charles."

"I want to let you know we hung your new work as the featured piece in the gallery. I put it dead center in the main room, visible from the street for all to see."

"That must mean you like it?"

"I think it's your best work. I'd like to do a one-woman show. What do you think?"

Charles could hear samba music playing in the background. Anise, short for Anisette and the only name she used professionally, hesitated before giving a response. Born in Bello Horizonte, Brazil, Anisette Nascamiento had migrated to America in her teens.

"Well, it depends. . .when. . .were you thinking?"

"I have an opening in November. . .and then one in February."

"Charles, that's. . .I could never be ready for a November opening, with all new work! How many do you want?"

"We could do it with twenty."

He scratched the dog curled up in his lap and toyed with a Mont Blanc pen on the desk, waiting for her to agree.

"Charles! There's no freakin' way I could do that in a few months. Are you nuts?"

He sniffed. "Alright, then, what would be reasonable for you?"

"Charles, I don't know. But twenty is out of the question."

"What would you say to fifteen?"

He waited, but she didn't respond.

"Okay, how's ten? Could you prepare ten new works?"

She inhaled and let it out in a rush of resignation. "I *could* do ten. . .I think. But not for November. Let it be February, but both of those months stink for openings, and you know it. What does my darling Vanessa say? She has a great feel for these things."

Charles ignored her question. "Can't fit it in any other time, Anise. But I can sell the hell out of them, and that's what counts. Just plan on being here for the opening and wear something appropriate, a black dress, perhaps, not those hippy overall things you wore to the last show."

"Thank you, Charles, I'll keep that in mind."

He glanced at his calendar. "I'll call you in the next couple of weeks. Do we have a deal?"

"Yes, Charles...and I'm *so* glad you like what I'm doing."

"I do, I do, indeed. Stay in that zone for this show, and don't deviate. I have some ideas on how to promote it. We'll talk."

He hung up without waiting for a further reply. Having achieved his goal, he sauntered into Vanessa's office. "I just got Anise to agree to a one-woman show for February."

"Dad, why February? That month is slower than a tortoise. What about the end of—"

"Because, m'dear, I have someone better in mind for that time of year."

Vanessa turned her palms up, shrugged, and waited for him to clarify the comment.

He smiled. "In time daughter. In due time."

She hated when he did that. She might be gallery manager, even the director, but she'd never be his partner—not in the true sense, not as a confidant or a joint decision maker.

Charles went to his office; Vanessa waited a few minutes, got up and walked to the doorway, turned to look at the large Anise painting, heaved a sigh, shook her head in disgust, and called to her father. "Dad, I'm going out for a few minutes."

She didn't wait for a response.

GALLERY 212 WAS ON DELGADO STREET, a short distance from the Hollingsworth Gallery, but barely visible from Canyon Road.

Bill Yarbrough sat thumbing through one of Santa Fe's ubiquitous free publications and glanced up when the motion sensor chimed.

"Vanessa, my love! How nice to see you."

Genuinely cheerful, he rose and greeted her with open arms. Close in age to her father, Yarbrough exuded a youthful enthusiasm, was well liked by other gallery owners, and had a reputation for being extremely knowledgeable, as well as reliable.

Tall, heavy-set, with a gleaming shaved head, he was wearing clogs, a billowy shirt with a silk scarf thrown around his shoulders like a prayer shawl, rings on all five fingers of his left hand, and diamond studs in both ears.

His gallery was tiny compared to the Hollingsworth; the works on view in the diminutive space were black-and-white photographs, with several by Robert Mapplethorpe, Diane Arbus, and Cindy Sherman.

The collection of the iconic image-makers fit Yarbrough's personal taste and lifestyle. 212's clientèle included entertainment celebs, a number of European and Asian collectors, and a handful of locals.

The gallery space was stark, with white walls, an ebony wood floor, and a few austere black benches and tables. On the wall opposite the entrance stood a narrow, matte black Parsons table with a crystal vase containing one brilliant red Amaryllis.

"What brings you here? Slumming?"

"No, my dear friend. I need a shoulder."

Bill stepped back and studied her face for a clue as to what was on her mind. "Well, what seems to be the problem? If it's a man. . . ."

She laughed and took his hand, pulling him toward a bench along one wall.

"No silly. Well. . .yes actually, but not a *boyfriend*."

"Oh, dear! Not that attractive, uber-hetero egotist father of yours?"

She sat on the bench and pulled a tissue from her purse, sniffled, and dabbed at the corner of her eye. "Sorry, Bill"

He waved her off. "Don't be. What's going on?"

"I don't know how much longer I can do this," she sobbed.

"Do wha—oh, you mean work with Daddy?"

"You are *so* perceptive." She said it with a note of irony.

Bill's face softened. "Seriously, love, talk to me."

"I have a masters in art history," she began, "I worked for three years at the Guggenheim, and I was assistant director at Gagosian in New York. I could get a job in most any gallery in America."

The words spilled out of her. "I know my stuff. . .and I wouldn't take the crap I get from him from anyone else in the world. What am I supposed to do? He never gives me credit; he won't let me make decisions and treats me like a child. I'm thirty-four fucking years old, goddam it."

She leaned back to rest her head against the wall.

Yarbrough patted her hand and then put his arm around her. They were silent for a minute before he spoke to her in a conspiratorial, avuncular tone. "You're right, darling, he should be ashamed, but that'll never happen, and we both know it."

Vanessa nodded and sat up straight. "I know he isn't even aware of it. It's just his way, but I can't go on like this. I'm wasting my talent, I don't have a life outside the gallery, and . . . ."

"Okay," Bill said, warming to the role of confidante.

"Let's say you left. Where would you go? What would you do?"

"That's just it, Bill. I *have* no place else. My stepmother Barbara is beyond being a lush. I can't even talk to her half the time. There's no man in my life. Or a woman, for that matter."

Bill turned toward her. "You don't mean—"

"Oh, Jesus, Bill, I don't mean *that*. I'm talking about friends. I work at the gallery six days a week, and by the time Monday rolls around, I'm worn out. I stopped going to the gym, I don't ride my bike, I. . . ."

"Hm. Why not take a vacation? Go somewhere, any-where. Just get out of here for a few days at least. Clear your head. Think about what you really want to do."

She hesitated, contemplating the idea. He could see she was working it over in her mind.

"I don't know," she finally said. "Maybe, but—"

"But nothing. Just go. Tell him you need some time off and leave."

"Where? Where would I go?"

"Oh come, dearie, there's lots of places. Cancun. . . Cabo . . .Belize? I know someone in Belize who has a waterfront *casita* you could stay in. He's never there this time of year. Walk on the beach. . eat fresh shell fish. . .cocktails at sunset."

"Sounds lovely."

"But what?"

"I hate to go by myself."

"Bring a book."

She looked straight ahead, wistful. "Maybe you're right." Then she brightened and exclaimed, "No, you *are* right. That's exactly what I need. I'll tell him today."

"You go, girlfriend!"

CHAPTER SEVEN

Bridge Over Troubled Water

KEITH ASKED TÉJA TO TAKE DEIRDRE to school so he could get to the gallery sooner than usual. As with most early mornings, Canyon Road was serenely quiet. The few people on the street were walking dogs or sweeping their sidewalks; some were at the Tea Shop picking up pastry and a cup to go. Keith bought a muffin and coffee, grabbed a newspaper, and then headed to Twin Angels.

A few minutes after ten, Paolo swept in and greeted him with a broad grin and hearty, "*Buon giorno, Padrone!*"

The artist was casual in demeanor and in his choice of clothing—paint-spattered blue jeans, a light blue denim shirt outside the pants, and a pair of beat-up running shoes with no socks. He had tossed a black sweater over his shoulders, the arms dangling loosely at his sides.

Keith offered a perfunctory, "Good morning," then pointed to his office. "Let's go in here."

Paolo sat across the desk from his benefactor, glanced around the room, but didn't look at him until Keith cleared his throat and pointedly said, "So, *Signori*. What can you tell me?"

Paolo scratched his cheek with one finger, took a breath and shrugged.

Growing impatient, Keith suddenly blurted, "*Paolo, basta*! Are we still working together or not?"

The phone rang before the painter could reply.

Not wanting any interruptions, Keith hesitated, but then seeing the caller ID, lifted the receiver.

"Twin Angels Gallery."

"Is this Mr. Wheeler?"

"Yes, may I help you?"

"Mr. Wheeler, this is Nurse Hayes at Crestone Elementary."

Keith's face drained of color. His stomach tightened. "Is something wrong with Deirdre?"

"I don't think it's anything serious, but she threw up in the classroom and is running a temperature. We prefer she be taken home as a precaution against anything contagious. You might want to take her to your own doctor. Can you come get her?"

He stared at Paolo, not wanting to put off the conversation. "Uh—is it all right if my housekeeper comes for her?"

"Is it a relative? We prefer that the parent do it."

Keith sighed heavily. "Never mind. I'll be there soon as I can."

He quietly put the phone down and turned to Paolo.

"Looks like this will have to wait. My daughter is sick, and I must go pick her up."

"I am sorry," he said, and seemed to mean it.

Keith was visibly dismayed, "I will call you soon as I can."

Rinaldi almost looked relieved. Keith was not. Concerned

for Deirdre and anxious about the artist, he felt terribly off balance.

They both stood up. Paolo sympathetically said, "I hope your child will be well."

"Thank you, Paolo. We'll talk later. *Ciao.*"

As soon as Rinaldi left, Keith turned off his computer and was about to leave a note for the gallery assistant when she walked in. "Hi, Sonya. Sorry, but I have to pick up Deirdre."

Sonya was in her early thirties, always dressed neatly, not unattractive, but not quite a looker either. She was very pleasant, great with customers, and understood the gallery business.

"Anything wrong?" she asked.

"Probably nothing more than an upset stomach. Anyway, take over, and I'll call you soon as I know more."

"Sure, Keith. Go. I hope she's okay."

He left through the courtyard door and drove to the school, a few minutes from the house. When he arrived, his little girl was sitting on a bench in the nurse's office, a thermometer sticking out of her mouth, her skin damp, her eyes glassy. The walls of the room, an institutional green, were adorned with posters—*Our Skeletal System, How to Perform CPR,* and *The Heimlich Maneuver.*

There was also a reproduction of Norman Rockwell's *Country Doctor.* Keith put his hand on her clammy cheek and smoothed her damp hair.

"Hi, honey, how'r you feeling?"

The nurse walked over and pulled the thermometer from the girl's lips. "I'm nurse Hayes. Are you Mr. Wheeler?"

"Yes." Indicating the thermometer. he asked, "What does

it say?"

Hayes squinted at the gauge. "Hm—a hundred and two."

He knelt by his little girl. "Okay, sweetums, we gotta get you home."

"Mr. Wheeler, will you please sign this release before you leave?"

The nurse, wearing a stiff white uniform with a pink sweater over her shoulders, seemed to be all business, but she had a caring smile and a concerned look on her plain, narrow face.

"Where?"

She handed him the clipboard, pointed to the signature line, and he signed the document without reading it. Still kneeling by Deirdre, he asked, "Do you want me to carry you to the car, baby?"

"I can do it, Daddy. Will you hold my hand?"

"Of course, honey." He hoisted her up. "Come on, let's go."

On the way home, he called the pediatrician and made an appointment to bring her right in, and then called Téja to tell her what was going on.

"*Ai, dio,*" she exclaimed when she heard.

"We're going to see the doctor, and we'll be home soon as we're finished. I'll call if anything changes."

"Thank you, Mr. Keith. I will pray for her."

"Thank you, Téja. But I don't think it's anything serious."

She rolled her rosary beads between her fingers and had her eyes closed. "I will pray anyway. *Adios.*"

"I know of a mumps case in Bernalillo," the pediatrician said. "But I don't think that's what this is. Her glands aren't swollen. It looks more like a flu or stomach virus. Let's watch it for the next day or two. Give her some ibuprofen, not aspirin, and no citrus juice. If her temperature gets above 102, or if her glands begin to swell, call me right away."

In the few minutes it took Keith to drive back home, Deirdre had fallen asleep. He called Paolo and told him to put off making any decisions until they talked. Although he didn't know for sure, his gut told him it was already too late.

He tucked the little one under the covers, gave her the pill, and put a cold washcloth on her forehead before darkening the room.

"Try to sleep, baby."

"Okay, Daddy. But will you stay with me until I do?"

"Sure, kitten."

He felt for swollen glands in her neck, put the back of his hand against her cheek, and removed the cloth from her head.

It was already warm. He placed a thermometer under her tongue, held her tiny hand, and winked. Thoughts of Rinaldi were no where in his mind.

He looked at the digital readout. "Well, it's 101—not too great, but better," he muttered.

He pulled the white wicker chair up to the bedside and held her hand. Deirdre slept for the next four hours, and when she woke the fever had dropped to 99.9. He gave her another IB tablet, and brought her some chocolate ice cream, which she took in tiny spoonfuls but didn't finish, and in a few minutes she was fast asleep again.

Téja spent the night on the sofa just in case Keith needed her, but also because she was worried. From time to time he heard her in the other room, mumbling the rosary. It spooked him to hear her drone like that, making him think his little child was worse off than she was.

During the night Deirdre woke every few hours, sweat-soaked and moaning. Téja washed her with a cool, damp cloth and changed her pajamas. By dawn, her temperature had dropped to 99°, and Keith fell asleep in a chair next to her bed.

CHAPTER EIGHT

Dark Clouds, Silver Linings

KEITH WOKE AT FIRST LIGHT, saw Deidre sleeping with her mouth agape, her hair damp and stuck to the side of her face, her pajamas sweat drenched. Téja heard him moving about the room and stood by the doorway.

"*Buenos*, Mr. Keith. How is the little one?"

They spoke in whispers. "She needs to be changed again, but I don't want to wake her. Let's wait until she gets up, and then I can take her temperature."

He put his hand on her forehead.

"She feels cooler. Probably sweated it out."

"*Ai, que bueno!* I will make some coffee."

"Thank you, Téja. Why don't you get yourself taken care of first, I'll put up the coffee."

"It is no trouble. You must be very tired."

"Thank you, it's okay."

Deirdre stirred from her slumber and opened her eyes.

"Hi, Daddy. Hi, Tay-ha. Am I still sick?"

Keith smiled at her and sat on the edge of the bed.

"Well, I don't know. How do you feel?"

"Um—" she swallowed— "I feel a little better."

"Good. How's your tummy?"

"It stopped hurting me."

"Let's take your temperature."

She lay back down, opened her mouth, and stuck out her tongue.

While they waited for the results, Téja got a cotton night-gown with a Little Mermaid print on it and placed it on the bed.

Keith grinned when he peered at the digital window. "Hm . . . it's almost normal. That's *great*, sweetie."

Téja approached the bed. "Here, little one, would you like me to put this on you?"

Deirdre nodded and sat up with her arms over her head. Keith shuffled to the kitchen and placed a handful of coffee beans in the grinder.

When he went back to the room, Téja had already run a washcloth over the child's body, dried her, and dressed her in the nightgown.

"Téja, if you'd like, you can take the day off. I'll stay home with Deirdre today."

"Don't I have to go to school today, Daddy?"

"No, sweetie, I think you should stay home today. . .maybe tomorrow, too."

Téja, satisfied with Deirdre's health, turned toward the doorway. "I know she will be well now, Mr. Keith. Tomorrow I will come early."

By late morning Deirdre had eaten some breakfast, slept more, and eventually wanted to get out of bed. Her fever was gone, and color had come back to her face. The doctor called to check on her status and said she could go back to school the next day, as long as her temperature was normal.

They played checkers, Go Fish, and, of course, watched *Frozen*. He carried her around on his shoulders for awhile, and they giggled a lot.

He thought of Paolo several times and knew he had to get back to dealing with the painter. In need of some respite, he called Moira and explained what had happened with Deirdre, but that she was already feeling better.

"It was only a fever," he said, "nothing to worry about. She'll probably go back to school tomorrow."

"I am so glad to hear that. Children bounce back so fast, don't they?"

"Yes."

"Have you spoken to . . .?"

"Paolo? Yeah. . .well, no. . .we were about to talk when the call came about Deirdre. I'll pick up with him tomorrow."

"Hm. I hope you don't mind me asking."

"No, it's okay. But you're the only one aware of it, so please don't say anything."

"Of course not."

"Thanks. I'll see you tomorrow, then?"

He put the phone down, thought about seeing her, and it lifted his spirits.

He brought Deirdre cookies and milk, and propped her up in front of the TV with a blanket over her legs, and then called Rinaldi.

"Paolo, it's Keith."

"How is your little girl?"

"She's much better, thank you. I will be in the gallery tomorrow. Can we continue our conversation then?"

"Yes, yes, we must. What time?"

"Three o'clock?"

"Okay. I will come at three."

Keith still had no idea what the outcome would be, but as the day progressed, he started to believe he was ready either way.

He returned to Deirdre, and even though she protested, he put her to bed at seven, as much for her benefit as his own. He was spent. By morning she was her effervescent self. Keith took her to school and then went to the gallery.

Primed and waiting for Paolo to arrive, he passed the time by going through his emails and checking the calendar for events he had planned for the Twin Angels over the next several months.

While he hadn't sent them yet, full-color invitations to a Rinaldi solo show were printed and stacked in the supply closet. He made a mental note to get rid of them, if it came to that.

VANESSA STOOD OUTSIDE HER FATHER'S OFFICE and tapped on the open door. "Dad, can I have a word with you?"

Charles didn't look up. "Sure, what is it?"

"Is it okay if. . . ." She stopped and started again. "I'm taking a few days off."

Charles looked over the top of his half glasses. "When? Why?"

"Soon. I just need some time for myself."

"You're all right, aren't you? There's nothing I should know about, is there?"

She remained outside the door. "I'm just feeling burned out, Dad. I want to take some vacation time."

"Is there a man?"

"Oh, Dad, if there was a man, maybe I wouldn't need a vacation!"

Charles' office was elegantly appointed and cozy. It boasted an authentic Louis XVI desk, a gold-and-maroon-striped satin settee, several 18th-century engravings, and a Daumier print. For Santa Fe it was a bit of an anachronism; there wasn't a hint of Southwestern decor in the entire office or the gallery, nor a touch of silver or turquoise anywhere. The building itself wasn't even adobe, but rather a stone facade, more Country French than Puebloan. Charles loved being different.

"Well, when did you plan to go? I am about to—"

"Dad, I'm going. I'm sorry, but I *am* entitled to time off. And I *am* taking it."

He stared at her, caught off guard.

Vanessa didn't wait for his response but went into her office and closed the door. She sat behind her desk, and her legs began to shake; her stomach was queasy.

She took several breaths and let them out slowly until she felt composed; then she picked up the phone and called Bill Yarbrough.

"Bill? It's Vanessa. I did it. I told him. No ifs, ands, or buts."

"Well, good for you. I'm proud of you. *Now* what are you

going to do?"

"I'd like to take you up on that offer and see if your friend's place is available. Would that be okay?"

"Honey, let me make a phone call and get back to you. When do you want to go?"

"I haven't really thought about that—it depends on when it's available and if I can stay there. By the way, what will it cost?"

"You know, I have no idea. I never paid to stay there. I only stay there with Felix. It's his place."

"Do me a favor—when you call, call me on my cell, okay?"

"Sure, I understand."

Charles knocked on her office door, entered without waiting, and sat in the arm chair opposite her desk.

"Vanessa. . .this is not a good time for you to be leaving."

"And why not, Dad?"

He cleared his throat and smirked at having to explain himself, least of all to his daughter. "Because it's just not a good time."

Not wanting to lose her momentum or high spirits, she gathered her courage and looked straight into his blue-gray eyes. "Well, Dad, if you won't share it with me. . .then I'm afraid it there's no reason for me to change my plans."

"You told me you didn't have an exact date. What difference will a few weeks make?"

"Probably not very much, but if I know the way things work around here, a few weeks will turn into a few months. And to tell you the truth, Dad, if I don't get away from here soon, I'm going to. . . ."

Her resolve was new to him, and he liked it almost as much as he didn't. "Vanessa, you're beginning to sound more like your father every day."

"I hope not," she muttered.

"I heard that."

She inhaled deeply and considered her next words. Charles observed her with an uncharacteristic sense of pride for the insolence she was showing.

"Dad, how about telling me what's going on?"

"In due—"

"You said that the last time. I need to know now…and not just because I want to take time off. You have to start letting go of the reins, Dad. I know what I'm doing. The gallery is my life. Actually, it's my *only* life right now."

"Oh, I see. So you think you should be running—"

"Dad! You're not *listening* to me."

He pulled back, his mouth partly open.

With each second that passed, the clock on Vanessa's desk clicked like a metronome. Along with the hum of her laptop, they were the only sounds in the room. Charles stood up and was about to say something, thought better of it, and walked out.

CHAPTER NINE

On The Cusp

PAOLO STROLLED INTO THE TWIN ANGELS GALLERY at exactly three o'clock. "*Ciao*, Keith!"

"Hello, Paolo."

"*La bambina?*"

"Better, thanks."

Keith offered him coffee.

"No, thank you. I have already too many espressos for today. I will not be able to hold a brush."

Keith gestured for Paolo to follow him to the office. They sat facing one another for a few moments before Keith asked, "So? Tell me, where do we stand?"

Reaching for Kendra's carabiner, Keith turned it over in his hands, waiting for a reply. Rinaldi finally leaned forward, scratched at his cheek, and cleared his throat. "I am sorry, Keith," he hesitated a moment before continuing. "I have decided to make a move."

There it was, the betrayal. Keith had been holding his breath, now he exhaled and repeatedly squeezed Kendra's climbing clip with his thumb and forefinger. The pronouncement hurt more than he anticipated.   "I see. To Hollingsworth?"

"Yes."

"Humph. . .well, then, there's not much more to say, is there?"

Rinaldi made signs of contrition, shrugged, and turned his palms upward. "It is just—"

"Paolo, it's okay. We have no written agreement. You have to think about your future, and I'm sure Hollingsworth has promised to do more for you than you think I can."

Paolo started to explain again, but Keith cut him off.

"No, my friend, there are no words you can say that will make it right. I will arrange to have your consignment works brought over to Hollingsworth. But. . .I hope you realize the door here is closed."

Rinaldi looked pained.

"Had you . . . had you spoken to me about this first, before making the choice to leave, perhaps we could have worked something out. Instead, you chose to deal behind my back. This is a small community, and little can remain a secret. Do not forget that, my friend." He rolled angry words around in his mind before deciding to be a gentleman and said only, "I wish you *buona fortuna* all the same."

Paolo rose, shook his one-time benefactor's hand, smiled meekly, and walked out. Keith watched until the painter had left the gallery and then slumped into his chair. Quickly glancing at the photo of Kendra, he swiveled around to look at the wall behind him with Deirdre's drawings and spotted the picture of himself and Castelli. It had been the venerable dealer himself who taught him the ebb and flow of the art business, and he nodded at the image and the memory. "Life goes on," he murmured to no one in particular.

MOIRA SLIPPED INTO THE TWIN ANGELS between the lunch and dinner hour. "Hi. How'd it go?"

"You were right. He's gone."

"To Charles?"

"Yes."

"That bastard!"

"Who? Charles or Paolo?"

"Both. The least they could have done was to tell you, so you could prepare."

Keith laughed at the assertion. "Moira, that would never happen. Why would they want to do that?"

"What did Hollingsworth offer him?"

They were standing in the center of the gallery. Sonya was out on an errand, and the place was empty of customers.

"Y'know, I didn't inquire, and I don't care. Paolo didn't ask if I would make a counter-offer, and as I told you before, I won't get into a bidding war. Life's too short."

"I admire your strength, Keith. What'll you do now?"

"You mean for a replacement?"

"Yes. Do you have someone in mind? Do you *need* anyone else?"

"Listen," he suddenly interjected, "I'd like to get out of here for awhile. Let's go for a walk?"

"Sure. But I have to be back for the dinner crowd."

While walking, she tucked her arm under his. She was

almost as tall as he was, and together they made a very attractive couple. Momentarily lost in their own thoughts, they walked along stride for stride until they got to a bench and sat down.

"So, what's your plan?" she asked. "Will you look for another artist?"

"I'm *always* looking for artists, but I have no one in mind right now. It's okay, really." He was putting on a good front. "I'm fine with it."

Moira studied him trying to read his handsome, youthful face. He didn't register a flicker of arrogance or concern.

"You're really serious, aren't you?"

"About what?"

"About not worrying that Paolo went over to the dark side."

He thought the reference was amusing and snickered. "So is Charles the Darth Vader of Santa Fe?"

"I've often thought he could be evil. Nefarious would be a better term."

"Interesting analogy," he chuckled. "Why do you think that?"

"There's something unsettling about Charles Hollingsworth."

"Like what? How well do you know him?"

"He actually reminds me of my ex-husband."

"Oh?"

They had never talked about her marriage.

She sighed. "He was. . .is. . .an entertainment lawyer in L.A. Arrogant, self-serving, rich, and verbally abusive."

"What happened, or shouldn't I ask?"

"No, you can ask, but we're here to discuss Paolo."

"You're right, we are. Let's stay on topic. We can talk about that another time."

Keith told her how he discovered Rinaldi's work and cajoled the Genoan into letting Twin Angels Gallery represent him in the States. Moira listened with great interest, but after a while stole a glance at her watch.

"I have to get back. I'm sorry. We'll have to continue this. Forgive me?"

They headed back to Canyon Road and stopped outside his gallery, where she leaned in and kissed him, a soft lingering kiss; before their lips parted, her tongue touched his for a split second, sending a wave of heat through his body.

"Soon," she whispered.

Walking to the Kiva, Moira looked over her shoulder before going in and saw Keith standing by the doorway of Three Angels, watching her, and then he waved goodbye.

Sonya came out from behind her desk and handed Keith a couple messages. "You had a few calls."

He shuffled through the pink notes and looked at the clock. "These can wait until tomorrow. Will you please lock up? I've got to get home."

"Sure. What's up with you and Moira?"

"What do you mean?"

"Well, for one thing, I never knew you to take off midday without someone being here to cover."

Keith shook his head. "Yeah, well. . .gotta go now."

She cocked one eyebrow at his response and laughed.

"Okay, then. See you tomorrow. Have a good night."

VANESSA LEFT WORK AFTER NINE that evening and drove to her condo on Bishop's Lodge Road. Halfway there, her cell phone rang.

"Vanessa?"

"Oh, hi, Bill. What've you found out?"

"Felix said he doesn't want to rent the place anymore."

She pulled off the road and stopped the car. "Oh, that sucks."

"Not all bad, actually."

"Why's that?"

"Like I said, Felix is a *very* good friend. So when I told him about you and that it would mean a lot to me, he said okay."

Her mood immediately shifted from dejection to elation. "I wouldn't want to put him out."

"Not to worry, dear. And here's the best part. He won't charge you anything. Just asked that you restock the bar and leave the place the way you found it. I assured him you would and gave him my personal guarantee."

"Bill, you are such a dear. How will I—"

"Don't worry, girl, I am thrilled to help. When you get back, we have to do lunch and talk about your future. Okay?"

 "Absolutely! I am so happy right now. Thank you. When is it available?"

"He has no plans to be there until Christmas. It's yours anytime between now and then."

Her mind was racing. "Thank you, Bill, thank you so much. I'll see what flights I can get."

"What else have you told your father?"

"Like I said, only that I was taking some time off. He was

speechless."

"Good for you. I bet your dashing dealer of a father was aghast at the audacity of it all."

"Dashing, indeed. He's going to find himself dashing around the gallery while I'm gone. Talk to you tomorrow, Bill."

It was almost midnight by the time she had searched flight schedules and finally made up her mind to do it. Booking the flight gave her the strength of commitment to tell Charles she was going, period.

She knew little about Belize, only that she could be there in about five hours, at least to Belize City.

She had no idea where Felix's place was located, other than an island called Caye Caulker, wherever the hell that was.

It had been a long time since she cast her fate to the wind, and the idea of a new adventure thrilled her. She googled *Belize* and thought it looked charming and exactly what she needed, the complete antithesis of the Hollingsworth Gallery and her aloof, domineering father.

She eventually fell asleep, but only after envisioning Mayan ruins, coral reefs, warm sand, a hammock, balmy Caribbean breezes, and the tropical sun bronzing her pearl white skin.

In the morning, she felt light-hearted and purposeful. She called Yarbrough and told him again how excited she was, and that she planned to go the following week. "Bill, tell me more about the place. This is so unlike me to do. Where is it, exactly? What about the key? Is there a grocery nearby? Do I need a car?"

"Not to worry. I'll write it all out for you. Just stop in later, and we'll get you all set."

"I'm gonna owe you big time"!

"Vanessa, it's my pleasure to help. You've been a good, non-judgmental friend to me, and you send buyers my way. I should be giving you a commission!"

"You just did. I'll come in around three, okay?"

"That's fine, darling."

A FEW DAYS AFTER THE PAOLO DEBACLE, Keith took a decidedly positive approach to the future of Twin Angels and sat down with Sonya to set things in motion.

"Sonny, let's go over a few things."

She poured herself a coffee, pulled up a chair, took a tiny bite of an almond croissant, and said, "Go!"

"First things first. Paolo Rinaldi will no longer be associated with this gallery. He's gone over to the Hollingsworth."

The look of astonishment on Sonya's face said it all.

Keith quickly reassured her. "Not to worry, we'll be fine, but I need your help gathering his sales history and the list of people who bought them from us. Then we need to have his work picked up by Hollingsworth, except for *Sunset 1* and *Memories of Genoa*. Those belong to me."

Sonya stopped taking notes and looked up from the legal pad. "Will you tell me what happened, or is it personal?"

"No, it's not personal. I'm not exactly sure whether Paolo sought out Hollingsworth or it was the other way around, but if I know Charles, he made the first move."

The door sensor chimed, and two people entered the gallery. Sonya looked up and greeted them. "Good morning. Welcome to Twin Angels. Feel free to look around. Let me know if you have any questions."

The couple was dressed casually. He was in slacks and an embroidered long-sleeve shirt; the woman, probably in her late fifties, wore jeans, cowboy boots, and a short fringed red leather jacket.

Her French-tipped finger nails were a quarter-inch long, and on one finger she sported a diamond the size of an olive. "Thank y'all. We'll do that," said the man.

Keith took notice of the man's Lucchese boots and the Rolex he was wearing and whispered to Sonya, "Let's continue this later."

He studied the couple as they moved through the gallery. At one point they stopped in front of a series of mono-print landscapes by a local artist, and Keith walked over.

"Hi. I'm Keith Wheeler, owner of Twin Angels. Do you have any questions or specific interests?"

The man put out his hand. "Name's Jessup, Roland Jessup, and this here's my wife Dolly."

Keith gave a slight bow of acknowledgment. "Pleased to meet you. Welcome."

Dolly turned her attention toward the group of prints on the wall. "What can you tell us about these?"

"Lovely, aren't they? They're by Joyce Gordon, a local artist. She works in mono-prints as well as watercolor. These images are of Pecos National Park."

"They're pretty," she said, and looked closer at them and then the price.

"Are these sold as a set, or can they be bought individually?"

"We'd prefer they stay together; they make more of a statement that way and complete the narrative, don't you think?"

Keith turned to look at the man. "How do *you* like them, Mr. Jessup?"

"In matters of art, I defer to Dolly. She's the artistic one in the family."

Keith switched gears. "Are you an artist, Mrs. Jessup?

"Call me Dolly. I am. Oh, not professionally, but I paint and sculpt whenever I can, which is never enough."

"Oh, she's just bein' modest," interjected Roland. "This here little lady is not only beautiful, she's a bundle of talent. Won best in show at the Cattlemen's art exhibit two years ago in Abilene."

"Congratulations," said Keith sincerely. "That is quite an honor."

"Yes, it was. Nobody was more surprised than me."

"Are you interested in seeing more of Joyce's work?"

Roland shook his head, "No, we'll take these, but I am interested in that Rinaldo fella you represent."

"Yes, of course. How do you know his work?"

"A friend of ours from Fort Worth has one."

"Fort Worth?" Keith paused momentarily, running the name through his mind. "Mm, that would be the Dickersons, right?"

Roland's face contorted in surprise. "Y'all know them? Shoot, of course you do. You sold 'em the dang thing."

"Nice people, the Dickersons. They fell in love with that canvas immediately and bought it the same afternoon. You must like it very much to come in and ask to see more of his work. How do you know the Dickersons?"

"Jack's the past-president of the Cattlemen's Association."

"Are you a rancher, Mr. Jessup?"

"Y'all call me Rollie, hear? And, yessir, my family's been ranchin' for more'n a hunnerd years."

"Well, let's take a look at what we have of Paolo's work."

He led them to the other side of the gallery, where three Rinaldi canvases hung. They were the pieces set to go to Hollingsworth.

"Take a look at these three. They're different from his more recent work, all of them important."

Dolly moved in to have a closer look and then studied smaller areas a little at a time. She moved from one painting to the other, and shook her head slowly side to side, and glanced toward the adjacent wall, where the two Rinaldi's that Keith owned were displayed.

"What about those? They're his also, aren't they?"

"You have a good eye. They're unlike his other work."

She peered at them, peeked at the descriptions and prices, and stepped back to take them both into her line of sight.

"These are wonderful! I like them better than *those*." She pointed over her shoulder. "Tell me about these."

"What do you like about them in particular?" He asked.

"I like them because they *are* different. It's not the same kinda painting Rosalynn has."

"You mean Mrs. Dickerson?"

"Yes, Rosalynn Dickerson. If I had one of them Rinaldi's, I'd want somethin' real special. They're not exactly cheap, y'know."

Keith didn't address her last comment, just nodded. "What else do you like about them?"

She turned to her husband. "Whatta you think, honey? You like 'em?"

"Like I said, darling', this is your department. I buy and sell beef on the hoof, whatta I know about art?"

"Well, now he's being modest. Roland knows more than he lets on. . .about most anything."

Keith was being careful with his pitch.

"Well, what do you think Mr. Jes—Rollie?"

"They're good. I like 'em, I guess. If Dolly does, they're okay by me."

Dolly placed a pair of half glasses on her nose and scrutinized both paintings, glanced around the gallery, and moved to another corner. Keith watched her, not sure where things stood.

Sonya approached the woman. "Mrs. Jessup, would you like a cup of coffee? We have some sweet rolls, too. . . . And you, sir, would you care for some coffee?"

"Not if you call me 'sir.' That's what I call my pappy."

Keith caught Sonya's eye, nodded for her to continue, and then said, "Would you excuse me a moment, I have to attend to something in my office. Please stay as long as you like, and please have some coffee. We also have San Pellegrino and soft drinks."

"Thank you," Dolly purred, "I'd like a coffee. . .black, please. Rollie, honey, what would you like?"

"I'm good, darlin'. You just go on doin' what you're doin' I want to talk to Mr. Wheeler here for a minute."

He took Keith by the elbow. "Like a word with you, Mr. Wheeler. If that's awright?"

"Certainly, come into my office."

He led him to the room and offered him a chair.

"What's on your mind?"

"Listen. . .we're celebratin' our twenty-fifth weddin' anniversary in two weeks."

"Congratulations."

"Thank ya'. What I want t' do is buy one of them paintin's for her without her knowin' it. Now, I need you to figure out which one she really wants."

He reached into his shirt pocket. "Here's my bidniz card. You call me and let me know how much I owe ya, and I'll wire ya the money. Then you send the picture to our home the day before our anniversary party. We're havin' a big ol' Texas bar-be-que."

He spread the word out so it took a few seconds to finish. "And I want that Ree-naldo to be there for everybody to see. Can y'all do that?"

Keith took the card, looked down at it and nodded.

"It would be my pleasure."

Jessup held a finger to his lips and clapped Keith on the back.

"It's our little secret, now, right?"

"Right."

When Jessup left, Keith shook his head at the absurdity of selling the painting and losing Rinaldi in such close proximity. Both paintings were marked at $25,900.

Keith had bought them for $5,000 each as a measure of

good faith when Paolo joined Twin Angels; since that time, the Italian's work had become a profit as well as a prestige builder.

It would be tough for the gallery not to represent him, and Keith knew it. He just didn't want anyone else to know.

CHAPTER TEN

The Send-Off

MARTA'S TELEPHONE SEEMED TO RING nonstop for two days following the gala. All were compliments and congratulatory messages. The prior evening's gala was only part of the tribute; most people were elated with the collection and its value to the community. For Marta it was a mixed emotion made palpable by the fact all of it would be cared for by the cultural center and that she could visit whenever the mood struck.

KEITH STEPPED BACK INTO THE CENTRAL GALLERY and found Sonya in front of the two Rinaldi canvases, quietly conversing with the Jessups. He listened to his protégé describe Paolo's work.

"…There is a passion exhibited in *all* his art, but these two give a glimpse into his personality in a way none of his previous work has."

"Paolo," she continued, "has undergone a great transformation, rather…an evolution in his work since living in America. And it shows. These two express it best."

"Which of the two do you think is the more successful?" asked Dolly.

Keith paid particular attention, listening for a clue to Dolly's preference, while Sonya, knowing it was probably the last chance to earn a commission on a Rinaldi, responded with more caution than usual.

"That's an interesting question," she responded; "Both of these express a new color palette. The brush strokes are longer, freer, and he used the palette knife less than he did in his earlier work."

Dolly stepped in to take a closer look, moving side to side, assessing the details Sonya had pointed out.

Roland turned toward Keith to see if he was listening and then, without his wife seeing, winked.

Keith gave Dolly a chance to process the information, hoping she would choose at least one of them, but, not wanting to disrupt her thoughts, he said nothing. Finally, after vacillating from one to the other, Dolly stepped back, focused on *Memories of Genoa*, and nodded several times. Keith came along side, and speaking very softly, said, "Are you favoring this one?"

"I do like it. It speaks to me; although I have never been to Genoa, there's something about it that's oddly familiar."

"Yes, I agree. . .I've visited there on several occasions. Rinaldi has captured the timelessness of a place that is steeped in history."

She looked again at the price, sighed, and stepped back to gaze at the image before turning toward her husband.

"Roland, honey. . .I like this one a lot, don't you? But. . .but it's a lot more expensive than what we thought."

Roland shot a glance at Keith and moved to where his wife was standing with a hand on her hip, her head tilted.

"Yep, it sure is a pretty picture. But you're right. Let me think on it a while, honey."

She squinted at the canvas for a few seconds, put her hand in Roland's, and whispered in his ear, and then walked over to the Joyce Gordon monoprints.

"I guess," said Roland, "we'll just take these for now."

"I can take care of it over here," said Sonya. "Did you want to take them with you, or would you like them shipped? You'll save on taxes if we send them."

"That'll be just fine," said Rolland. "Ain't nuthin' wrong with savin' a little money. Is there?"

"I'll need some information to complete the sale and write up an invoice. Will you be paying by check or credit card?"

"Cash, darlin'. You do take cash, don'tcha?"

"It comes to a total of $3,490, including the shipping cost!"

Keith cleared his throat. "Sonya, we'll cover the shipping costs, no charge to the Jessups."

The cattleman pulled an enormous cylinder of bills from his pocket, undid the rubber band holding it together, and proceeded to count out thirty five one-hundred dollar bills. "That should do it." He rolled up the remaining wad, replaced the rubber band, and shoved it back in his pocket.

Sonya's eye had widened at the sight of the cash, but she didn't skip a beat as she went about completing the sale.

Keith shook Jessup's hand and said, "It's our pleasure to work with you both. Thank you for your business and interest."

He turned toward Dolly and held out his hand. She reached for it, and he cupped it with his other hand and then thanked her.

"Enjoy the Gordon prints, and thank you for stopping in. Let us know when you will be coming this way again; perhaps we can have dinner."

"That'd be real nice, Keith. Thank you."

When the couple left the gallery, Sonya turned to her boss and said, "I really thought they were going to buy the Rinaldi."

"They did."

"What?"

He had a wry smile on his face. "Roland told me he'd take whichever one she liked the most and to ship it to them for their anniversary next week."

Sonya grinned. "Well, well, well…what a send-off for Signori Rinaldi. It certainly has turned out to be an interesting day."

Keith touched her shoulder, "Nice job selling it Sonya. That was a well-deserved commission."

Vanessa steeled herself for a confrontation about taking time off. She sipped her coffee while applying eye-liner and then dressed slowly, selecting an ankle-length rust-colored suede skirt with a high slit up the side and calf-height boots, topping her outfit off with a brown cashmere cowl-neck sweater. Her hair was pulled back in a French braid.

She drove directly to Yarbrough's 212 Gallery and parked on Acequia Madre, so she wouldn't be seen by any one at the Hollingsworth.

Yarbrough was at his desk, his red-framed half glasses pushed down almost to the tip of his nose, a gold-link chain holding them around his neck. He was wearing black leather pants and black velvet bedroom slippers with a gold monogram.

"Hi, Bill."

"Well, if it isn't our lady of the arts! Don't you look stunning."

"Thank you, Bill. Love your pants."

"Gautier. I bought them in Paris—aren't they marvelous?"

"I'm sorry to be in such a rush, Bill, but I want to get back before Daddy gets there."

Yarbrough returned to his desk, picked up a manila envelope and handed it to her.

"The key is in here, along with directions to the house from the airport. You'll need to take the water taxi, which runs in conjunction with the airline schedules. There's a list of bars, restaurants, and the location of the grocery-liquor store. You just have a good time, sweetheart, and if you go to the Turtle Inn, be sure to give my regards to that gorgeous bartender Shiloh, and let him know I sent you."

He put his arms around her and gave her a giant bear hug and two air kisses.

"Tah-tah."

Vanessa let out a sigh of relief, her eyes moistened momentarily, and she said, "Thank you so much, Bill. This is such a wonderful gift."

Feeling exhilarated along with a touch of anxiety, she drove to Alameda Street and then back to the Hollingsworth, so it would appear she was coming from home, more to protect Yarbrough from her father's wrath then worrying about Charles' response to her taking time off.

Madeleine and Dennis were at their desks, sipping lattes, when she walked in.

"Good morning, guys."

"Morning, Vanessa."

"Is my father in yet?"

Before either of them answered, Charles called out. "I'm in here."

She stepped into his office, repositioned an antique chair, and sat down directly in front of him, feeling a little as if she were in the principal's office and not with her father.

"Dad, I'm going away for a week."

"You already told me that."

"Well, I said I *wanted* to, but I hadn't made definite plans."

"And now you have?"

"Yes."

"I see. And when exactly do you plan to do this frivolous thing?"

"Call it what you want, but I am leaving next Thursday."

"Don't you think it would have been a good idea to share this with me before you made arrangements? And where are you going, by the way?"

"What does it matter where I'm going, Dad? You run the gallery anyway, I'm just a figurehead. Madeleine and Dennis will be here, so you don't need me."

He sat back, studying his daughter—how much she looked like her mother, how much she reminded him of her tough exterior and level-headedness, and now how she was standing up to him, which he hated.

"Vanessa, darling, I told you this was not a good time."

"Oh, Dad, when would it ever be a good time?"

"Well, if you had come to me to discuss it, perhaps we could have found one together."

"Doubtful," she mumbled.

He ignored the comment and continued to speak at her, rather than to her. "I have been working on a very exciting deal."

"That's exactly my point. I am never included in your—" she made little quote marks in the air with her fingers— "*deals*! I find out about them only after the fact. I have no say."

"Vanessa, you are just like your mother."

"I take that as a compliment." She looked away from him, feeling frustrated and hurt. "Dad, stop dancing around and start talking to me like your partner first and your daughter second. I'm not your little girl anymore."

He took a breath, and a tiny, almost imperceptible, smile began to form before he altered his tone of voice. "No, you're not. I can see that. And I also hear that. Good for you for standing up to the ol' man."

Ignoring his tiny acquiescence, she asked, "So are you going to tell me about this deal?"

Charles reached for his glass of water, took a swallow, and then drew his lips together in contemplation, cleared his throat and leaned forward. "This goes no further."

"Of course."

"We are now representing Paolo Rinaldi!"

He was clearly impressed with this pronouncement...and it showed. Vanessa took a few seconds to process the information before responding. "*That's* newsworthy. When did it happen? I don't know what to think. I mean, how did it come about? How long have you been planning this?"

"Vanessa, darling, that's not important. What is important is that he's on board."

"Well, I suppose congratulations are in order. He'll be a great addition to our portfolio—but I wonder what the street will say about us stealing him away from Keith."

"That is of little concern to me. And if my guess is right, they'll all be envious."

"Perhaps, but a lot of our reputation comes from how we treat artists and clients as well as how we're viewed by our competitors."

Charles waved it off. "I frankly don't care what the competition thinks."

His cavalier response was another point of difference between them, but she held back saying anything.

"So," he continued, "now you understand why I don't want you to leave. There's a lot of work to do. We need to promote the hell out of this and set up his first solo show for a big opening. I want it here before we do the Anise show."

Her shoulders became uncomfortably tight, and the hollow sensation in her stomach made her want to throw up.

"Well, Dad, it'll just have to wait until I get back."

Almost horrified by his daughter's new-found grit, he sat back and scowled. "Vanessa!"

"No! You are *not* going to do this to me. Rinaldi can wait.

And if it can't, then *you* take care of it."

She stood up to leave.

"What is this, mutiny?"

"Call it what you want, Dad. I'm going on vacation."

She wavered slightly when turning to leave but held firm, left his office, went to hers, and closed the door.

A minute later Charles knocked. "Vanessa, you left this 212 Gallery envelope in my office. Is it for me?"

CHAPTER ELEVEN

Better Late Than Never

MARTIN PAINTED ALL AFTERNOON and, when finished, moved the work aside, futilely swept the dirt floor, straightened up the studio, and prepared yet another blank canvas with a layer of gesso. He worked incredibly fast, and his output was prodigious; a cache of finished work lined every available space, silent reminders of his efforts and his hidden talent.

He took a quick look around the dimly lit studio, smiled ever so shyly, walked to the house, set the table for supper, and waited for the family to get home.

NOT QUITE SETTLED DOWN from their adventures at school, twelve-year-old Verdad and eleven-year-old Maya ate and chatted animatedly throughout dinner.

"So, t-tell me about school t-t-today," Martin asked.

Verdad, mouth full of rice, raised one finger, but before she could swallow, Maya spoke up. "I made a new friend today."

"That's good, little sister," said Russell. "Tell us about her."

"It's a *boy!*" shouted Verdad, rice sputtering from her lips.

"And he's in the seventh grade."

"Let *me* tell," cried Maya, "It's *my* friend. You're just jealous."

"Hardly. He's not even cute."

Martin and Russell both suppressed a laugh.

Téja wiped her mouth and said, "Tell us about your friend, Maya." Then she turned to Verdad. "And *you* don't talk with food in your mouth."

Maya was excited and spoke quickly, afraid Verdad would interrupt her. "He's really nice, and he's smart, and. . . and—"

"And how did you meet him?" asked Russell.

"In math class. . .he sits next to me."

"He's not so smart," said Verdad.

The sisters bantered back and forth until Maya fell silent and the older one knew it was time to stop teasing her.

"I'm just kidding," she assured her. "He *is* nice. And kinda cute, I guess."

Maya grinned and went back to eating.

"Russ, how d-d-did the book rep-port, go?"

"Good, brother. I got a 'B'."

He raised an open hand, and Russell reached across the table to smack it with his.

Téja leaned over and took hold of Martin's hand.

"What is this on your hands?"

Martin turned both hands over and looked at them.

"Paint."

"Maybe you should clean them before dinner, no?"

"No, Auntie, I am going back to do some more. I will clean them later."

"Don't go to work like that tomorrow. They will fire you."

"I would not d-do that, Tía, y-y-you know that."

She gazed at him, knowing how meticulous he was, and that he was also afraid to let anyone know about his art.

"If they knew you were such a good painter, maybe you wouldn't have to hide it. Maybe you would not have to wait on tables."

Martin shook his head.

"M-maybe I'm not such a good p-painter."

"You are blessed, Martin. You must believe in yourself and in *Jesús*."

"I believe in Him, and He will let m-me know when it is t-t-time."

Téja patted his cheek. "All right, then—" she motioned to the others— "it is time to clear the table and do your home-work. Whose turn is it to wash the dishes?"

"My turn," said Russell.

"Tía, I want to go back and p-p-paint. Do you need me to d-do anything?"

"No, Martin. But don't stay up so late; you have to work tomorrow."

"G-good night, everyone," he called over his shoulder as he left the house.

"Good night, big brother."

MARTIN FELT AS THOUGH THE PAINT was cooperating with every stroke of the brush. He worked steadily—controlled and focused, in that sacred place where artists and athletes can do no wrong, when every move, every gesture, flows like an invisible current, infusing them with a confidence and ability beyond the normal range of skill.

The night was silent, except for the occasional high-pitched yelping of coyotes. He had the radio on, but the sound was so low he hardly noticed the static. Hours swept by without his being aware of anything; he was at one with the painting.

Energized by the surge of creativity, he didn't tire until almost dawn, and rather than wake the household, he curled up on a mat in the corner of the studio and plummeted into a deep, heavy sleep that even the crowing rooster didn't disturb.

When she noticed he wasn't in the house, Téja sent Russell to look for him, and he found him asleep there. He went back to the house and told his aunt.

"*Ai, pobrecito,*" she said. "He works so hard. . .but I have to wake him, or he will be late. Russell, get yourself and the girls ready for school."

Téja wiped her hands on her flannel robe, threw a sweater over her shoulders, and trudged across the backyard to the studio.

She knocked on the door and when there was no answer, she knocked harder and called out, "Martin, *joven.* Wake up!"

Martin bolted and scrambled to the door.

"Ay, dio, I f-fell asleep. What time is it?"

"It is late. Look at you—you are covered in paint."

She shuffled back to the house without another word.

He had to wait until everyone was finished before he could get into the bathroom. He looked in the mirror—smudges of green and yellow paint on his nose, cheeks, forehead, on his hands, and under his nails.

He hurried back to the studio, poured turpentine on a rag, began scrubbing at the stains, and then went back to shower; but by then, the water was so cold he could only stand under it for a few seconds, so he did the best he could to get cleaned up.

He hastily put on his white shirt and black pants, and raced to catch the bus, missed it by a minute, and stood watching helplessly as it trundled down the road. The next wouldn't come for an hour. He stepped off the curb and stuck out his thumb.

It was almost ten minutes before the driver of a rusty pickup truck stopped and gave him a ride to Santa Fe, dropping him near the interstate. Martin hitched another ride a few minutes later and got close enough to walk the rest of the way. It was 11:40 when he walked into the café, sweaty, frazzled, and out of breath.

Cydney had completed setting the entire dining room, Peter was standing behind the bar, and Moira was by the podium. She looked at the shy, disheveled figure standing in the entrance.

"Martin, are you okay? What happened to you? You're a mess."

"M-m sorry," he said, his hands shoved deep in his pockets, his hair damp and hanging over his forehead.

"It's okay, you're here now. We'll talk later. Please get cleaned up and ready for lunch."

He hustled to the men's room and did the best he could to cool down and look presentable.

WHILE MOIRA WAS AWAY from the entrance, a family of five sat down at one of his tables. The children were noisy and fidgeting; the father pretended not to notice and perused a tourist guide while the mother glowered at the boy playing with the sugar packets and growled at the girl sitting on her knees facing backward on her chair.

"Betsy, turn around and sit right. . .and you, young man, stop playing with the sugar. Hal, do something."

Her husband looked up.

"Whatta you want me to do? Leave them alone. They're not bothering anybody."

She smirked and looked around the restaurant.

"Where's our waiter? We've been here for—"

"Pris, give them a chance. They just opened."

He looked at the kids. "Does everybody know what they want?"

Martin came out of the bathroom and went directly to the table.

"Hello. My n-name is M-Martin. Are you r-r-ready to order?"

The kids giggled. Pris shot a glance at her husband and then glared at her children.

"I want a cheeseburger," demanded the girl, "and fries!"

"They don't have cheeseburgers, Bets. This isn't Wendy's."

The girl pouted and crossed her arms.

Her brother stuck his tongue out and snickered.

"Never you mind, Brian," admonished his mother. "You just worry about yourself. What do you want to eat?"

"There isn't anything to eat here."

Pris glowered at her husband. "I told you we shouldn't have come here. It's too good for them."

Her husband sighed, put his arm around his son's shoulder, and lifted the menu.

"Okay. Let's see what we can find for you and your sister."

Martin waited patiently, expressionless, until they finally selected something, and then went into the kitchen to place the order.

The woman watched him disappear behind the door. "Did you see his fingernails?"

"No, Pris, I didn't. What's wrong with them?"

"Wrong? They're *filthy*. You'd think the restaurant would check their people before letting them wait on tables."

She looked around, caught Moira's attention, and motioned for her to come over.

"Yes, how can I help you?"

"Are you the hostess?"

"I'm Moira, the owner. Is there something wrong?"

"I'll say! For one thing, you don't have a children's menu."

"I'm sorry. No, we don't."

"Well, it doesn't matter now—and don't you check your wait staff to make sure they are clean before they serve customers?"

"Our staff is very professional. We've never had any complaints. What seems to be the—"

"Our waiter, the one that stutters. . . ."

Moira winced.

"His fingernails are filthy. And how can you hire someone

with a speech impediment to wait on customers?"

Moira was on the verge of losing it and felt an instant dislike for the woman. She was about to ask them to leave when she saw the bartender watching the exchange.

"I apologize. I'll have Cydney take over your table. Would that be alright? And I'll have a look at Martin. Sorry for the occurrence. Let me offer you complimentary dessert and beverages."

She didn't wait for a response, but turned and walked into the kitchen.

"Go-Go" was standing at the center island where orders were placed for pick up.

"Martin, can I see you for a minute?"

"Yes, M-ma'am. What is it?"

"Martin, may I have a look at your hands, please?"

He hesitated briefly, then sheepishly held them in front of her with his palms up.

"No, dear the other side."

He turned them over and held them out, shaking as if they were going to be smacked by a nun's ruler.

"I'm s-sorry. I c-c-couldn't g-g-get..."

She took his hands in hers, turned them over and back again.

"Martin, what were you doing? Painting your house?"

"Uh. . . ."

She let go of his hands. "Never mind. Get some scouring powder from Jerry, and see if you can't get them clean. Thank goodness it's slow today."

"B-but I have c-c-customers—"

"Cyd'll handle it. I can't let you serve like that."

He looked as if he were going to cry.

"Martin. It's okay. They'll get clean, and you'll be fine. Don't worry about it."

The door swung open, and Cydney entered the kitchen and began calling out orders.

"Cyd, can I see you for a minute."

"Sure, what's up?"

"I need you to cover for Martin. I'll give you a hand."

"Is he okay?"

"Yes. He just has to take care of something for me." Cydney nodded. "No worries. I'm on it."

MARTIN WAS REASONABLY SUCCESSFUL getting the paint out from under his nails. By three-fifteen the restaurant had emptied out and Moira called him into her office. It was barely a room —more like an alcove, crammed with a small metal desk pushed against one wall, stacked with two wire trays, receipts, invoices, and produce orders—barely big enough for the computer monitor and telephone. Moira was sitting in a straight-back chair next to a black metal file cabinet. Martin squeezed in and leaned against the door frame.

She pushed some papers aside, placed an elbow on the desk, and rested her hand under her chin, her fingers pensively pressed against her lips.

"Do you want to tell me about this?"

Martin's face flushed, but he gave no response. Moira waited, giving him time to collect himself, and seeing that he was reluctant to speak, she rifled through some papers and pretended to be distracted while waiting for him to say something.

"Am I go-g-going to be f-fired?"

She looked into his large, dark brown, calf-like eyes.

"No. No. . .oh, Martin, no. I just want to know what happened. You are always spotlessly clean and a wonderful waiter. I have nothing to fire you for."

He looked around for someplace to sit, leaned against the file cabinet, shoved his hands into his pockets, and heaved a great sigh.

"I o-o-overslept." He didn't mention his hands.

"It happens. But what about the paint?"

He winced and looked at the floor.

"Martin, are you in some kind of trouble?"

"N-no."

"Then what's going on?"

He saw the compassion in her eyes and, for the first time since art school, decided he would let someone else know about his obsession.

"P-please d-d-don't tell anyone. Okay?"

"Okay."

"Uh, um. . .I p-paint at night."

"You have another job?"

"N-no. I paint. . .p-pictures."

Moira's mouth hung open slightly and she blinked a couple times, trying to understand what he meant.

"What kind of pictures? You mean. . .art?"

"Yes."

". . .That's *fantastic*, Martin. I didn't know that. Why do you keep it a secret?"

It was difficult enough for him to hold a lengthy conversation, but talking about his art was out of the question. Moira could see he didn't want to discuss it, so she let up on him.

"Well, I think that's terrific, and you should be proud. Maybe someday you will show them to me."

"Th-th-thank you, M-m-m. . . ." He stopped short of finishing, pulled his hands out of his pockets, folded his arms, and looked at the floor again.

"Well, you have time before we open for dinner. Make sure those hands are clean, and we'll keep this between us, all right?"

He nodded sheepishly several times. "Th-th-thank you."

CHAPTER TWELVE

Making Appointments

FLUSH WITH HAVING SUCCESSFULLY wooed Paolo Rinaldi to his gallery, Charles was in a celebratory mood and not about to let Vanessa's impetuousness upset him. I'll deal with it when she gets back from wherever she's going, he thought.

Reaching for the phone, he tapped in Paolo's number. The phone rang several times before the answering machine kicked in and, although he preferred to talk to the artist directly, he reluctantly left a message.

"Paolo, it's Charles. I'd like to finalize our agreement and talk to you about having a gallery reception. Call me."

He slid the desk drawer open and removed a four-page legal document—a party-of-the-first-part, party-of-the-second-part- style contract—scrutinized the content line for line, and made notes next to a few sentences as he went along. Satisfied with the changes, he reached for the phone again but this time pressed a speed dial number. After four rings, he was about to hang up, when a groggy voice answered.

"H-hello?"

"Oh, Jeez, Barbara are you still sleeping? It's almost noon."

"Charles? What do you. . .why are you calling me?"

"Actually, I wanted to share some news with you."

Barbara sat up and shoved a pillow behind her head. The sheet dropped away, exposing her naked body, and, catching a glimpse of herself, she brought her knees to her chest, pulled the comforter around her shoulders, fumbled for a water glass on the nightstand, and slumped back onto the pillow. The room was dark, the shades down, and the curtains pulled closed. Her jeans, shoes, and blouse lay in a pile on the floor; her lacy Cosa Bella bra hung over the arm of a chair. There were no panties.

"News, huh? What could you possibly want to share with me?"

"How about meeting me for lunch?"

Perturbed, she growled, "Why don't you just tell me on the phone?"

"Barb, I didn't call to get into an argu—" He could hear her light a cigarette and take a deep drag. "Oh, never mind, it's spoiled now."

"Oh, stop. If you have to see me to tell me, it must be important. You're not getting married again, are you?"

He laughed, guffawed actually.

"*No*, I'm not getting married. It's about the gallery, and I wanted to tell you in person, that's all. Forget it."

"Hmph. Okay. Where, and what time?"

"How about La Fonda at two? That'll give you some time to get ready."

She hesitated, thought about it for a moment, and replied,

"Fine. I'll see you there."

She threw the covers off, stretched, yawned, swung her legs over the side of the bed, and stood up. Switching on the table lamp, she looked in the mirror and instinctively cupped her breasts in her hands, lifting them so they were higher. She smirked and turned so she could see her backside, sighed, shrugged, and sashayed into the bathroom, where she squinted at her reflection.

Fingering the puffiness under her eyes, she grabbed a tube of Preparation H and dabbed it on to bring the swelling down. On the counter, surrounded by jars of cream and make-up, along with mascara smudged cotton balls, sat a coffee mug containing an inch of vodka, a remnant from the night before. She stared into the cup for a few seconds and then downed it.

Sitting on the edge of the tub, she ran her trembling fingers through her tangled hair while a tear slowly made its way down her cheek.

BY THE TIME MARTIN GOT HOME, he was exhausted. The day had worn him out. He slogged into the house and found everyone had gone to sleep except Téja. She was watching television and sewing the pocket of Russell's jacket.

"*Ai, niño*, you look so tired."

"I am, T-Tía. It was a hard day."

He bent down to kiss her on the head and then slumped onto the sofa next to her.

"Do you want something to eat, Martin?"

He let out a huge, exasperated sigh.

"I can't keep p-painting at n-night. I d-don't know what

t-t-to do."

"But you can't stop painting. You love to paint. I don't know about art, but I know your things are beautiful. I see the paintings Mr. Keith has in his home. One time he showed me the place where he works. There are many art things there. Your paintings should be there, too."

Martin stared into space, his hands limply at his sides.

"*Pobrecito*," she said, "I will go to bed so you can sleep now."

Barely able to keep his eyes open, Martin nodded in agreement. "Good n-n-night, Tia."

He fell asleep in his clothes and slept so soundly he hardly moved; awakening at dawn, he managed to get into the shower before anyone else did.

He dressed quietly and set the table for breakfast, then he knocked on the bedroom doors to wake the others and waited until he heard stirring from the girls and a sleepy, "Good morning," from Russell. He walked across the yard and into the studio and studied the paintings on the easels and against the walls. He crouched on the floor, grabbed a fistful of dirt, and let it slip slowly through his fingers like hourglass sand.

He then looked toward the ceiling with tears in his eyes. "Please, Madre, p-p-please. . .tell me what to do." He spoke in a hoarse whisper, his voice cracking with emotion.

Téja came to the doorway and beseeched him, "Come, *joven*. Breakfast is on the table."

He wiped his eyes with the back of his hand and stood up. She could see that he was hurting and understood it was not her place to ask, but her heart ached for him. He put his arms around her, pressed his face against the warmth of her cheek, and held her close without uttering a word. Téja felt his tears but didn't want to embarrass him, so she continued to embrace him in silence until he composed himself.

"Come. Eat breakfast with your family," she said.

Martin was quiet at the table, spooning the cornmeal cereal into his mouth without a word. The girls sensed something was wrong and kept their usual lively chatter to a minimum.

Russell kept glancing at Martin, but also remained quiet. Verdad and Maya cleared the table and kissed Martin good-bye before they and Russell left the house; Téja lingered at the table. "What is bothering you, *joven*?" she beseeched.

Martin, deep in thought, blinked and looked at his aunt.

"You are r-right, Tiá, I don't w-want to stop p-painting, but I cannot do b-both. Working at the K-Kiva is too impor-tant. We need the m-m-money."

"I understand, *hijo*. Pray to the Virgin, she will help you find a way."

"I will, Tiá. I will ask her. I will g-go to Saint Francis and l-l-light a c-candle and say the rosary."

She smiled, put on her coat, kissed him on the forehead, and left the house. Martin left a half-hour later and went to work.

CHARLES PULLED INTO THE PARKING GARAGE at La Fonda and paid the attendant extra to ensure the car was close to the entrance and away from other cars so it wouldn't be nicked.

He went inside the hotel, bought a *Wall Street Journal*, and sauntered into the restaurant, where the maitre d' rushed to greet him. "Mr. Hollingsworth, nice to see you, sir. Your table is ready."

"Hello, Roberto. Nice to see *you*. Are things well with you and your family?"

"Yes, sir. They are all well, thank you. And you? Your daughter? She is well?"

Not wanting to make more small talk, he answered abruptly. "Yes, we are both well. Has Ms. Dearborn arrived yet?"

The man seemed confused for a moment, and then his face brightened. "No, she has not come in. This way, please."

Closely following him to the dining room, Charles whispered, "Roberto, see to it that the wine list is left off our table."

As he had hoped, the dining room was quiet and only a few patrons remained. He looked at his watch, saw that it was exactly two o'clock, smiled at his own punctuality, and unfolded the newspaper.

It was two-fifteen when he looked at his watch again and then searched the entrance for Barbara. Her tardiness was always an issue for him. By two-thirty he lost his patience and angrily tapped at his phone. Barbara's handset rang several times without a response; not even the answering machine kicked in. He tried again in fifteen minutes before, exasperated, he stood up and left.

The valet had parked the car by the exit ramp; Charles handed him a ten and then drove to the gallery, stormed into his office, and closed the door. He tried calling Barbara one more time, got no response and slammed the phone down.

KEITH PUT ON A WHITE SHIRT, tan slacks, a blue blazer, and a pair of dark brown suede loafers; his thick, sandy colored-hair was combed, but casually.

"You look nice, Daddy."

"Thank you, sweetie. You be good now and go to bed when Cassidy tells you to."

Turning back to the television, Deirdre raised her hands over her head and wiggled her fingers good-bye. Keith pulled her up and gave her a hug, kissed her, and put her down.

"I'll see you in the morning, honey. Cass, I should be home by ten-thirty or eleven. Thanks again for doing this."

"No problem, Keith. I'm happy to do it. You just have a good time. Who's the lucky girl, Miss Lindstrom?"

He smiled broadly and winked. "See ya later, Cass."

She turned her attention back to the TV, calling over her shoulder, "Enjoy."

He got to the restaurant a few minutes early and waited for Moira by the entrance. She soon appeared in a black, scooped-neck, knee-length dress, and had on heels and a single strand of pearls; her hair was down, within a few inches of her shoulders.

"Whoa!" he said. "You look fabulous!"

She laughed that throaty, almost lusty laugh he had grown to love. Within seconds, the owner of the venerable establishment exclaimed, "Moira! It is so nice to see you. You look more beautiful than ever."

Keith was sure Moira blushed.

"Aldo! Good to see you as well."

"So business is good for you?" he asked her.

"Yes, no complaints."

"For us," he said, eyes rolling upward, "business is always good."

Aldo was a small man, with a dark Mediterranean complexion and the gestures and elegance of an old-world aristocrat. His eyes sparkled with the delight of someone who truly enjoyed life and people.

He turned to look at Keith. "I am so sorry. How rude of me."

Keith smiled and shook the man's hand.

"Keith Wheeler. Twin Angels Gallery."

"Yes, of course, but it has been a while. I was at the reception for, uh. . .Paolo Rinaldi. How is he doing? A great artist, no?"

Keith winced, then quickly recovered. "We're no longer associated."

Aldo was courteous enough not to pursue the obvious, and said, "Please come with me. . . . I give you the best table in the house."

He did, too, one in front of the fireplace, where they could see the front room but still have some privacy.

The converted old house had an understated elegance and European charm along with a hint of garlic and fragrant sauces simmering in the kitchen. Aldo returned to the table with a bottle of Barbaresco.

"With my compliments. Welcome back, Signorina."

He ceremoniously opened the bottle, placed the cork on the table, poured a tiny bit in one of the glasses. Then he held it up to the light, gently swirled it around to coat the edge of the goblet and let it slide to the bottom. He handed it to Keith.

Keith sipped it gingerly, allowing it to sit on his tongue before swallowing. Moira eyed him carefully while he went through the ritual, a tiny smile in the corner of her mouth. He nodded at Aldo, who smiled with approval, poured more into the two glasses and then said, *"Buon appetito!"* and backed away.

"Charming and not too pretentious," said Moira.

"The wine or Aldo?"

"No, you," she smiled.

"Actually it's a very nice wine. But you know a lot more about wines than I do. I mean, being in the business and all."

"Oh, I learned about wines in California. . .when I was married. My ex thought of himself as an oenophile and invested in vineyards in Sonoma and Napa. I learned about it so he couldn't con me with more of his high-and-mighty bullshit."

Keith leaned back against his chair. "Sorry. Didn't mean to touch a nerve."

"No, no, I'm sorry. Anyway, I do know a little, it comes in handy at the Kiva, but I hate all the pretense."

Keith took note of it—her comment about her ex, the way she explained herself without making an excuse, her self-assurance without conceit.

"So what *do* you think?"

"About the wine?"

"Yes."

She licked her lips. "Delicious."

Aldo returned to the table to personally make recommendations and take their order; Moira spoke to him in Italian.

Keith then asked questions in a flawless Milanese dialect, and Aldo was beside himself with glee.

Moira leaned in toward Keith. "Don't tell me you went to Italian cooking school, too."

"No, I studied art history in Rome and worked in an art gallery in Milan, and then was assistant curator in a small museum in Florence."

"Now, I'm really impressed. . .and embarrassed."

"Why?"

"I had no idea you were. . .your art background is understandable, but living and working in Italy—you're just full of surprises."

"Not really. We just haven't gotten to that yet."

She tilted her glass toward him, then sipped its contents ever so slowly, peering over the top of the glass while coyly studying him. Her eyes reflected the warm amber glow of the fire. She looked so very soft, almost ethereal, and very beautiful. He wanted to stroke her face, hesitated a second, then slid his hand across the table and touched the tip of her fingers with his own.

Although barely touching each other, the energy was tangible, and they continued to look into each other's eyes until the waiter set their dinner plates on the table.

Halfway through her tortellini, she put her fork down, dabbed at her lips with the napkin, and cleared her throat. Keith raised his eyes to look at her and rested his utensils on the dish. "What?"

"You haven't mentioned Paolo."

"Do we really have to?"

"Not if you don't want to."

He took a sip of wine and sat back.

"Okay. I've been trying to reconcile it in my mind. And I still get caught up in the way it was handled. I'm not sure I . . .well, I don't blame Paolo. I probably would have done the same if I were him. It's just the way he did it. I mean, considering how much effort I put in. . . ." He trailed off.

"Understandable, Keith. But tell me what you think about Charles. How unprofessional was it to steal Rinaldi right out from under—"

He waved it off. "I wouldn't expect less. It's just business to him. I don't even think he cares about the art. It's the idea that someone like me. . .that I had Paolo before he even knew the guy existed."

She watched him carefully, looking to see how hurt he was, if he *was* hurt. He lifted his fork to resume eating, but she interrupted him.

"What do you think you'll do? I mean. . .do you expect to find a replacement for him? And what are you going to do about Hollingsworth?"

"There's little point in me approaching Charles. Wouldn't make a difference anyway, because I didn't have a contract with Paolo. As for replacing him. . . ."

"Will it affect your business, if you don't mind my asking?"

"I'd like to think not, but yes, it will."

In that instant, she thought of Martin and wondered how good an artist he was. Keith could see she was in thought and waited a moment before asking, "Where'd *you* go?"

She shook her head. "Oh. . .sorry. . . nothing. I was just

thinking of a possible painter, but I don't know anything about him, so let it go."

He did, and they returned to their dinner, ordered two cappuccinos and one tiramisu between them. A little small talk over coffee segued to Deirdre and then to Kendra and his life after she died and whether he thought of remarrying, but he hesitated long enough for her to say, "We don't have to talk about it, if you'd rather not."

"No. I'm okay with it now."

His mouth formed a half smile, but he averted her eyes, brought the cup to his lips, then put it down.

"Yes, I've thought about getting married again, but. . . you know, you're the first woman that I found attractive and interesting, someone I wanted to know better and spend time with, I just wasn't sure how to go about it. Having a kid and all, I mean."

She reached across the table to hold his hand. "How soon after the accident did you start dating?"

He shrugged at first and then sheepishly said, "I guess it was about a year, a woman my neighbor Cassidy fixed me up with. Nice enough and fairly good looking, but my heart wasn't in it. I. . .I wasn't ready. Then a few months later, a woman I met—" he laughed— "in the supermarket."

Moira raised her eyebrows and giggled. "In what section?"

"Is that important?"

"Just wondering. It seemed funny."

Keith chuckled, "I think it was in the produce section. We went out for coffee a couple times, had a few laughs, and then discovered we were both widowed. After that, all we could talk about were our deceased spouses, and it got really weird...and made me sad."

"And then what? When was the next?"

"You."

"Really? That was only a few months ago."

"Yes, I know. I was despondent for awhile and figured I'd just never go out on a date again, or ever fall in love and get married."

He looked around, scanning the restaurant, and then glanced to the side to see who was sitting next to them. Finally saying, "Moira, I am very attracted to you, but. . . ."

"But what?"

"I am just getting used to the idea that you are in my life, but I don't know how you really feel, and if—"

"You mean if I feel the same way about you? Or about your having a daughter?"

"Both."

She gazed into the fireplace and got lost in thought as if it were the first time the idea had crossed her mind. Keith wondered if he might have pushed the limit and was about to change the subject when she turned back toward him and looked directly into his eyes, once again taking his hand in hers. "Okay Keith, here goes. I love that you have a daughter, and that you are such an amazing dad. I love our time together and wish we had more of it. . .I am *very* attracted to you and yes, I'm falling in love with you." She inhaled. "Okay, so how was that? Clear enough?"

He broke into a big grin and kissed her hand. "Yes. Clear."

They both understood saying anything more was unnecessary. After paying the check, they walked arm in arm to her car. She leaned against the door and Keith took hold of her hands, gently pulled her toward him, and then kissed her sweetly. She responded by kissing him passionately and long.

He eventually let go, took half a step back, and peered intently into her eyes but said nothing. She returned the gaze, her lips slightly parted, her face flushed.

"I love the way you kiss," she whispered.

"You, too," he said.

"Good night, Keith. Get home safely."

"And you, too. Watch out for the coyotes."

He waited until she drove off before walking to his car.

CHAPTER THIRTEEN

Taking Care Of Business

VANESSA WAS SITTING IN HER OFFICE, fretting over having left the Gallery 212 envelope on her father's desk. Charles, preoccupied with being stood up by Barbara, had all but forgotten it. She finally knocked on his door and poked her head inside.

"Dad, got a sec?"

"What is it?"

She could see he was distressed.

"...Please don't make such a big thing out of this. I'll be back in a week and we can—"

"I wasn't even thinking about it."

"Then what's troubling you? You look upset."

"Barbara didn't show up at our lunch appointment."

"And that's unusual how? And why were you meeting her in the first place?"

"Good question. I guess I wanted to let her know about Rinaldi. I thought she..." He shrugged. "It doesn't matter. She probably passed out."

Vanessa suddenly felt pity for him and stepped further into

his office. "Why do you allow her to. . .she's totally unreliable. All she does is hurt people."

"I know, but I feel sad for her and get to thinking about what we. . .what it used to be like."

"I'm sorry, Dad, I know you don't want to hear this—"

"Well, then, don't say it."

Just for a moment she thought he was going to cry, and it cut into her; there might still be a spark of humanity, some humility, in the man, after all.

"Okay, then," she countered, "I just came in to let you know my schedule."

"Um-hum."

"I'm leaving Thursday morning, and I'll be back in the gallery the following Friday."

"Where are you going?"

"Belize."

He sat up straight. "Really, how'd that come about?"

"Bill Yarbrough."

"Yarbrough. *That* queen? What'd he have to do with it?"

"Nothing, really," she lied. "He knows someone who rents a place on the beach and put me in touch with them. That's all."

Charles considered it for a moment but was still too caught up in Barbara's disappearing act.

"Well, just leave the information with Madeleine."

She gawked for a second and shook her head. "Nothing about 'have a good time' or 'I'll miss you'? Nothing? Just 'leave the information with Madeleine'? Dad, you can be so self-centered sometimes."

"Have a good time. I'll miss you."

Hurt and frustrated, she somehow managed to hold herself together and walked out.

HOURS EARLIER THAT DAY, Barbara continued to sob on the edge of the tub until she ran out of tears. She stood up, teetered for a moment, walked naked into the kitchen, opened a cabinet door, took down a bottle of Gray Goose, cracked the seal with shaky hands, and poured three fingers' worth into a dirty glass from the sink.

She took a single ice cube from the fridge and plopped it into the vodka, swished it around with her finger, took a swallow, and dialed the phone. It rang four times.

"Is this my sexy painter?"

Paolo yawned, "Who. . .oh, Barbara, *buon giorno*."

"Can I come over?"

The pause on the other end of the phone suggested more than she cared to know. She took another swallow from the tumbler.

"Are you alone? Never mind. . .don't answer that."

She could hear him breathing and imagined his tousled hair and sleep-swollen face and, for a moment, wanted to mother him.

"Yes, I am alone. What is it?"

"I just want to see you, that's all."

Another pause.

"I woke you. . .didn't I? I'm sorry. Go back to sleep. I'll call you later."

"No, *cara mia*, it's alright. I have to get up anyway. I have a meeting to go to. I was painting last night, so I did not go to sleep until three in the morning."

She tried again. "Can I come over? I'll bring lunch."

He sucked air in through his teeth. "Barbara, I must leave soon," he lied. "There's no time. *Domani* is good, yes?"

"No. I need to see you now!"

"I cannot. I call you later. *Ciao.*"

He hung up before she could respond. She slammed the phone down, flung the glass across the room, and started to cry before it even shattered against the wall. She fell face down onto the bed and sobbed vehemently for a few minutes, then got up, returned to the kitchen, grasped the bottle in one hand, her fingers clasped around the long neck, and shuffled back to the bedroom.

She took a long swig, coughed twice and dribbled some of the vodka down her chin, felt it trail between her breasts and pool in her navel. She ran her fingers along its path, licked them, took another swipe at the bottle, and crashed onto the pillow with a thud.

LIVID OVER BEING STOOD UP, Charles hesitated to meet with Paolo that evening as they had planned, but he picked up the phone and called anyway. "Paolo? It's Charles Hollingsworth."

"*Ai, Padrone. Tuto bene?*"

"Yes, fine. I am calling to confirm our dinner meeting. Have you reviewed the paperwork?"

"Yes, I be at your house at seven."

"Excellent. I look forward to it. We have much to do,

Ciao."

Charles put the phone down and immediately felt better, knowing business was running smoothly, Barbara all but forgotten for the moment. He tidied his desk, went into the gallery, looked around, entered Vanessa's office, and sat down.

"I wanted to let you know I'm meeting with Rinaldi tonight to sign the contract. By the time you get back from—where are you going again?"

"Belize," she smirked.

"Right, Belize. Anyway, by the time you get back, he will be part of this gallery, and I plan to feature him. I want to move the Anise and put up some of Rinaldi's work. I'm scheduling a reception for him in two months."

"That's nice," she said sarcastically.

Charles pressed his finger to his lips, waiting for her to say more. She looked at him without a hint of emotion. He took it as a sign of acceptance, nodded a few times, and rose from the chair.

"Well," he said, "I'm off. See you tomorrow. Have a nice evening."

HOLLINGSWORTH'S HOUSEKEEPER FIONA prepared *carne asada* for dinner and set the dining room table with festive Southwestern colors, turquoise and orange napkins, place mats decorated like Navajo rugs, candles set in clay pottery.

Charles studied the table setting for a few moments, selected some CDs from the wall unit, and went upstairs to change his clothes.

He came down half an hour later in blue jeans with knife-edge creases, a gray cashmere V-neck sweater, a white button-down shirt, and black loafers.

Paolo arrived promptly, and Charles met him at the door. "Welcome. Please come in."

They cut through the living room to the patio and sat facing the setting sun. Charles had had Fiona pick up some Moretti beer, and Paolo's eyes lit up when he saw the bottles chilling in a bucket.

"Ah, how do you know *birra d'Italia?*"

Charles smiled, pleased with his choice. "I thought you might like it. It's a good beer right?"

"Yes, it is from Italy. . . ." Rinaldi took a bottle in his hand. "You see this man on the bottle? He looks like my grandfather, Carlo Rinaldi Domiani."

Charles pulled one from the bucket, pried the cap off, and tilted the bottle toward Paolo.

"Have a seat. Enjoy the sunset."

They peered across the hill top as the sun slowly melted across the horizon into hues of amber, red, orange, and purple, crisscrossed by streaks of pink.

Paolo interrupted the reverie. "I have tried to paint the sunsets here, many times, but. . . ." He shrugged and took a sip of beer.

"Most artists who come here have tried," offered Charles, "but no matter how good they are, there is nothing that comes close to the real thing. Do you agree?"

"I will be the first!"

Charles smiled at his brashness. When dusk had over taken the view and the air grew cool, Fiona appeared on the patio and announced dinner.

Paolo eased himself out of the chair, stretched his slender frame, and stroked at his chin. Charles put his hand on his shoulder and led the painter into the dining room. "Have you eaten *carne asada*?"

In the center of the heavy dark wood table Fiona had placed a round woven basket filled with soft, warm corn tortillas and covered them with a cactus-pattern cloth.

Glazed azure-blue dinner plates sat alongside a matching covered serving bowl containing the shaved beef and spices. When Charles served, a piquant aroma filled the air. "Paolo," he said, "take a tortilla from the basket and put it on your plate."

He spooned a large helping into the center of the tortilla, and Paolo leaned over it to savor the aroma. "Mmmm, lime.. . garlic. . .uh. . .cumino, yes?"

"Very good, my friend. You know your spices. What else?"

Paolo leaned over the plate, cupped his hand, and brought the steam toward his face.

"Uh. . .cilantro, yes?"

"I am impressed. How is it you know these things?"

Paolo was clearly delighted with himself. "The nose paints pictures," he said. "Close your eyes, and you can still see the taste."

He tilted his glass toward the painter, took a sip, and then served himself. Paolo watched to see how his host wrapped the *asada* in the tortilla and followed suit.

They made small talk until they were finished eating and Charles suggested they move to the living room for coffee. The room contained several Breuer chairs and a Knoll sofa as well as a classic black leather-and-rosewood Eames chair and ottoman. The coffee table was glass and chrome, with a stack of art books and a brightly colored Lino Tagliapietra glass vessel on top.

The housekeeper brought a tray with coffee and biscotti, set it on the table, and left without a word. Charles sat in the Eames lounger, reached for the documents on the side table, and handed a copy to the artist, who was sitting on the sofa. "You've seen these already, but we should talk about them before you sign."

Rinaldi flipped quickly through the three pages and put them on the arm rest. "I had no contract with Twin Angels."

"That's true, but this is the way I do business and one reason why I am so successful."

Paolo surveyed the room with his eyes; he reached for the art books on the table, pushed the glass vessel aside to see the titles, then took a short sip of espresso, sat back, and cleared his throat.

Charles gave him a few moments, but the painter didn't say anything else.

"So, Paolo, do you have any questions?"

Rinaldi looked around the room again, lighting on the paintings, two by Anise, and a small bronze sculpture. He pointed to the latter. "Is original Brancusi? I think yes—why not, you are rich man."

Hollingsworth unconsciously drummed his finger before reaching for his coffee. He dipped the tip of his biscotti into the cup, bit into it, sat back, and crossed his legs. For a moment only music from the CD player could be heard, and then Paolo finally spoke.

"I understand that the gallery will get fifty per cent of my sales. I also understand that you will. . .how do you call it. . .*market* my work? That is all good, and I agree. But for the show each year I cannot promise so many paintings you ask for."

Charles listened intently for what could be negotiated, what he should concede, and what needed to be revised.

"Do you have concerns about anything else?"

Paolo picked up the papers and looked through them more closely. "Here—" he pointed to a paragraph on the third page—"you say I cannot be represented by another gallery."

Charles remained seated, showing no sign of concern. "Is that a problem, the representation?"

"I do not know how much you will sell. How can I. . .*limit* is the right word, yes?"

Charles waited.

"How can I limit to one gallery?"

"Well, what do you want then? I require exclusivity."

Rinaldi furrowed his brow at the word.

"Paolo," Charles explained, "I want my gallery to be the only one carrying your work. It makes it even more special, and we'll get people from all over to buy the paintings. We can demand a higher price. Don't you see?"

"No. I want to show in other places. I can not be in Santa Fe only."

"Where do you want to show?"

"Roma. . .Milano. . .London. . .New York."

Charles exhaled, clasped his hands behind his head, and closed his eyes.

A Brahms symphony finished and another CD started; Cuban music by the Buena Vista Social Club. The tempo was faster and upbeat, refocusing the energy in the room.

Charles took a deep breath. "Okay, my friend, here is my idea. You can show anywhere in Europe you want. But the Hollingsworth Gallery will have exclusive rights to represent you in the United States. Agreed?"

Paolo hesitated and slowly shook his head.

"What's wrong? If you show your work in other galleries, it becomes too. . . too available."

"Perhaps, but I don't know how many paintings you will sell here. I need to know I can sell other places in America."

"Paolo, if you cannot give me the number of paintings I asked for, how will you do them for other galleries?"

"That is why I can do only. . .um, maybe ten for you."

"I was hoping for twice that many."

"I know, *padrone*, but. . .we will start with that. Yes?"

"You drive a hard bargain, my young friend. . . . Here's what I will agree to."

Paolo leaned forward on the sofa, took a sip of coffee and replaced the cup on the saucer.

"If you find representation outside America, then you can have that—but no galleries in New Mexico, Arizona, Colorado, Utah, or Texas. Agreed?"

"I can be in New York and Los Angeles?"

"Only if our agreement is for three years. . .unless I terminate it with thirty days' notice."

Paolo tugged at his earlobe and thought for a few seconds. "Now you make the bargain, yes?"

Charles laughed, stood up, and held out his hand, "We have a deal then?"

Paolo grinned broadly, and their eyes met. "Yes. We have a deal."

"Good! Come to the gallery tomorrow afternoon, and we will sign in front of a notary, and then we will make an announcement. Let us toast?"

Charles poured grappa into two shot glasses, handed one to the painter, and said, "*Salute!*"

"*Ciento anni!*" added the painter.

CHAPTER FOURTEEN

Detours

KEITH WAITED UNTIL DEIRDRE had gone to sleep and Téja went home, and then he called Moira. "Hi! Are you still okay for Monday night?"

"Yes."

"I just got some tickets to the Aspen Santa Fe Ballet."

"That's wonderful. How did you score those?"

"Marta."

"How sweet!"

"Yes, I know. I put her in touch with an art appraiser a while back. She owns an original El Greco and is considering bequeathing it to a museum."

"She is such a special lady, isn't she?"

"One of a kind, to be sure. I'll pick you up at five. The performance starts at seven-thirty. We can have an early dinner beforehand."

After they hung up, Keith stood by the phone trying to absorb the heightened feelings he was having for her. A few miles away, Moira was doing the same.

WITH THE AGREEMENT SIGNED, Charles wasted no time contacting the Twin Angels Gallery. Keith was caught off guard hearing Hollingsworth's voice, expecting he would have had his daughter Vanessa or an assistant do the deed.

"Hello, Charles. What can I do for you…as if I didn't know?"

Charles sniffed. "Yes—well, I have no doubt you are disappointed."

Keith clenched his jaw, thankful they were separated by a telephone, and immediately changed his mind about dropping off the art.

"Listen," he said, "I'd like you to pick up Rinaldi's work. They're large, and I need the space."

Charles remained smug. "When would be convenient?"

Never, you supercilious bastard, thought Keith, before adding, "Today. They're in my store room."

"How many are there exactly? I think Paolo told me five. Is that right?"

"Three, actually. I own the other two."

"Oh, wise purchase, Keith. You do know good art when you see it. Well, since we are neighbors of sorts and not too far away, I'll pick them up in the van and not bother crating them. Say…five-thirty?"

"That'll be fine."

Keith hung up without saying good-bye.

"Sonya! Can you come in for a minute?"

She appeared at the doorway seconds later. "What's up?"

"Hollingsworth will be here at 5:30 to pick up the paintings. I want to move them into the storage area."

"Consider it done."

"Let's do it after lunch. I hate looking at bare spots on the wall, and I need to figure out what to put in their place."

"Do you have any thoughts on bringing in a new artist?" she asked. "Or is it too soon to think about?"

"Not sure. There was a woman featured in *Southwest* magazine about two months ago I thought was interesting. She isn't represented here that I know of."

"What kind of work?"

"She does non-representational and semi-realism. A very bold style, strong colors, works with a variety of tools."

"You mean Deborah Tremain?"

"Yes! Exactly. What do you think?"

"I think she'd be great!"

"Does she have a website?"

"I googled her after I read the article, but I couldn't find a dedicated site. She's mostly linked to galleries that carry her work."

"Which galleries?" he asked.

Keith went to his file drawer and thumbed through some papers looking for names.

"Never mind," said Sonya, "I'll find it."

While she searched, Keith took the two Rinaldis he personally owned, leaned them against the wall where he thought they would look best, and then walked around deciding what else to move.

"I got it!" shouted Sonya.

He went to her desk and looked at the monitor.

"Hey, she's way younger than I expected. Does it say how old she is?"

"She graduated from the Denver Institute of Art in '96."

"I was expecting someone older."

Sonya looked at the image again.

"Why'd ya think that?"

"There's a maturity to her work. I really need to see it in person, but from what I saw in the magazine and online. . . ."

Sonya glanced at the artist's photo again, scrolled through some of the pictures of her work, and turned back to Keith.

"I'll print out some of these images and download the contact info so you can email her."

"Where does she live?"

"Her studio is in Loveland, Colorado."

"Is there a phone number?"

"Yup."

PAOLO WAS ELATED with the new arrangement and wanted to celebrate. The moment he swaggered into his studio he pickled up the phone and called Barbara. While he waited for her to answer, he smiled at his reflection in the mirror, brushed his hair back with a free hand, and winked at himself.

The phone rang several times without a response.

Paolo shrugged and put the phone down, walked to a liquor cabinet and poured a glass of limoncello, toasted himself, and drank it in one swallow.

Sitting on the sofa, he surveyed his studio: one painting on the large heavy easel, two stacked against a wall, and several, unfinished, nestled in a rack.

One he was working on was only partially filled in; blank canvas showing through in spots, unresolved sections waiting for his hand.

Restless for companionship, his usual desire to paint was overwhelmed by a craving to engulf Barbara Dearborn in his arms and feel the wetness between her thighs, the tangy perspiration between her breasts, the feel of her lips on his mouth and on his body. He sighed at his own impetuousness and reached for the phone again, but, frustrated by the sixth ring, slammed the phone down and walked out of the studio.

Across town, Barbara finally woke to the jangling phone and, lying on her stomach, face mashed into the pillow, grappled for the receiver but couldn't reach it and sat up with great effort. Unable to focus through her blurred vision, she fumbled for the phone—but by the time she put it to her ear, the caller had hung up.

Exasperated, she threw the remote across the room, shattering its plastic housing and exposing the hanging battery pack and wires like disemboweled road kill.

Hung over, no food in her belly, she started to dry heave, but couldn't make it to the bathroom and fell to the carpeted floor on her knees, the room spinning around her.

Paolo stood in his courtyard, hands stuffed into his pockets, a cigarette poking out of his mouth, smoke drifting back into his dark eyes, causing him to squint.

Growing more irritated by the minute, he pulled at the cigarette and flicked it across the terrazzo tiles. His mood had gone from celebratory to exasperated in a matter of minutes, and he cursed Barbara for her reliable unreliability—and himself for letting it get to him.

CHAPTER FIFTEEN

Starts And Stops

MOIRA AND KEITH TALKED NON-STOP to Albuquerque and all through dinner. During the ballet, she held his hand from start to finish, and by the last *pas de deux* she had her head on his shoulder. On the ride back, Keith asked what she thought of the performance.

"I loved it, particularly the new works, very energetic. What'd you think?"

"I'm no judge really, but it was fascinating."

"This was fun. Thank you for taking me tonight."

"I'm really enjoying us, Moira."

"It's strange how long it took us to connect."

"Timing, I guess."

As the lights of the city disappeared behind them, they drove under a canopy of stars so vast it was like a celestial dust storm.

By the time they pulled into her driveway, it was after eleven.

"Would you like to come in?"

Keith reflexively looked at his watch. The thought of

being with her, just the two of them, was rare and enticing.

She leaned in and kissed him; then she reached for the door handle and stepped out of the car. He followed her to the house, their footsteps crunching on the gravel as they moved in the semi-darkness until a security light switched on. Moira opened the door slightly and knelt to keep the cat from escaping. She scooped her up and stepped inside, hit the dimmer switch, put the cat down, and turned toward Keith.

He encircled her waist with his arm, drew her closer, and pressed his lips to hers, increasing the intensity of the kiss until she slowly pulled away.

"Come sit in the living room," she suggested. "Would you like something to drink?"

"Nothing, thanks."

He sat on a pillow-laden contemporary sofa and was immediately joined by the plump, gray-and-white Selkirk Rex, who made it known she wanted to be stroked.

"Bruleé! Off!" commanded Moira.

"It's okay, she's fine."

"She knows better. She's taking advantage of you. Besides, *I* wanted to sit there."

She moved the cat to the floor, sat down and pulled off her shoes, and leaned back, absent-mindedly twisting strands of her hair around two fingers; then she abruptly stood up.

"Let me put on some music, and I'll be right back."

She nudged her shoes under the coffee table with her foot, moved silently across the floor to the credenza, turned on a CD of Pedro Romero playing *Recuerdos de Aranjuez*, and disappeared into another room.

Several minutes later, she returned wearing an oversized sweatshirt and jeans.

"Sorry. I couldn't stay in those clothes a minute longer."

She sat down and propped her legs on the coffee table, put her head on his shoulder, and closed her eyes. He studied her long slender fingers, clasped them in his, and kissed them very gently; she snuggled closer.

He could feel the fullness of her breasts against his arm and realized she had removed her bra; instantly he felt himself quiver at the thought of her naked.

Touching her hair, lured by its thick, silky texture, he couldn't keep from burying his face in it. The scent of her intoxicated him. She kept her eyes closed while, only a few inches from her mouth, he explored her features. Her breathing was soft, and he could feel it on his face just before he again touched her lips with his.

Her arms instinctively went around his neck, and she pulled him toward her as he searched for her tongue with his own. They kissed hungrily for several minutes until he thought his heart was going to careen through his chest.

Her breathing accelerated and came in short bursts when he slipped his hands under her shirt, down her back, and then to her breasts.

She let out a tiny gasp and pushed him back but held his hands against her and looked into his eyes with a hint of desire. Then, in an instant, she grasped the corners of her shirt and pulled it over her head.

He kissed her lips and fondled her again, taking her nipple into his mouth and gently wetting it until she began to moan.

She burrowed her face in the nape of his neck and kissed him there, letting her tongue slide along its length from his ear to his collar bone, and back again. He was electrified; his hand began to grope at her face, her shoulders, between her breasts.

She slid her hand under his shirt and felt his muscular back; inching her fingers down his spine, she came to his belt and tucked her fingers into the top of his waist band.

He found the snap on her jeans and undid it; she pulled up and looked at him, her eyes wide with longing.

"Let's go into the bedroom," she whispered.

She said it so low he wasn't sure it was what he heard, but then she stood up, took his hand and led him silently up the stairs.

The room was large, with a queen bed and a brass headboard; a dozen colorful pillows in different shapes lay on top of bolsters; a down comforter was folded at the foot. The walls were a salmon color with no decoration except for a French Impressionist painting above the headboard. In the center of the duvet was. . .Bruleé.

Moira lit a few candles, undid the zipper of her jeans, let them slide down her slender legs, stepped on the cuff of one side, and pulled them off with her other foot. Entranced, Keith watched quietly, his heart pounding as his eyes lit on her lavender thong, which she hooked with her finger tips, pulled down and gently kicked aside. She stood there in the candlelight, totally alluring and absolutely certain that he knew it.

She stepped toward him, reached for his shirt, undid the buttons and pulled it off; then she tugged at his trousers until he assisted her in removing them.

They embraced and fell backward onto the bed, the cat scurrying to get away before being squashed. In seconds their bodies were entwined, arms and legs wrapped around each other like the boughs and branches of some exotic tree.

The heat of their bodies reached a fever pitch, her skin, dewy and wondrously scented, filling him with a yearning that suddenly catapulted him to thoughts of Kendra.

He squeezed his eyes shut, buried his head between Moira's breasts, and held her tightly, pressing her against him so there was no space between them from their shoulders to their knees. As he entered her, he felt the heat inside her and they moved together in an undulating rhythm until all of his emotion exploded in a rush of lust, lost love, and his rediscovered virility.

VANESSA WAS THREE DAYS INTO HER TRIP before she could thoroughly enjoy the relaxation or the tropical heat and the total change. Ultimately venturing to the Turtle Inn, recommended by her gay confidante, she sat at the bar and ordered a Mai Tai, sipped at it slowly, and then ordered another.

The girl behind the counter, a Guatemalan beauty, brought the drinks within minutes, each time flashing a glorious smile.

"My name is Bonita," she said, when she delivered the second drink. "What is yours?"

Struck by her friendliness and stunning looks, Vanessa didn't hesitate. "Vanessa!"

"*Buenos*, Vanessa, *bienvenidos!*"

Vanessa smiled then inquired, "Is—does Shiloh still work here?"

The young woman looked puzzled and she hesitated for a moment before responding. "*Ai*, you mean *Esheelo*. Do you know him?"

"We have the same friend."

The girl nodded and left to attend other customers.

A few minutes later, a slim, dark-skinned man with jet black, shoulder-length hair slid behind the bar, patted Bonita on the rump, and adjusted the white short-sleeve shirt hugging his torso. The first four buttons were undone, revealing a large gold medallion. Bonita motioned with her head toward Vanessa and, when he glanced her way, she assumed it was Shiloh. He came directly to where she was perched on the rattan barstool.

"*Hola!*" He put out his hand. "I'm Shiloh." His English was virtually without an accent. "I understand we have the same friend?"

"Yes, he asked me to say hello."

Shiloh nodded, waiting for more.

"Bill Yarbrough."

Shiloh momentarily pursed his lips, then made the connection. "Ah, Bill. The art dealer. Charming man…dangerous, but charming."

Vanessa was curious about the "dangerous" part but didn't inquire.

Her eyes moved from Shiloh's face to the silver-dollar-size religious medal of the Virgin de Guadalupe. When she looked up, his eyes were fixed on her. In that instant, she realized he was as straight as could be, and that he was just an unfulfilled fantasy of Bill's. With looks like a fashion model and the swagger of a high-school quarterback, it was no wonder. Her pulse quickened when he smiled again and winked at her; then he took hold of her glass and said, "Allow me to get you another drink. . .um?"

"Oh, sorry. It's Vanessa."

"A beautiful name."

"Thank you, but I've had—"

He slid away before she could protest or decline the third drink, or anything else.

The bar sported the requisite palm frond canopy, several rattan bar stools, a few low cocktail tables with small glass candle holders wrapped in plastic netting, hibiscus floral print easy chairs, and tiki torch lights. Beyond lay the beach, its expanse of white sand, and the placid turquoise water of the Caribbean.

She scanned the endless horizon, took a deep breath of sultry air, and waited with some trepidation for her drink. He soon appeared with a tall, frosted glass, placed it in front of her with a flourish and pronounced, "A Tai for. . .your sunny smile. This one is on me."

Even though it was apparent he was an enormous flirt, she flushed, and knew that he, not Bill, was the dangerous one.

As she sipped the sweet concoction, she watched people casually stroll in and take the remaining seats at the bar and tables.

Obvious honeymooners smooched and touched and giggled at a far table; a middle-aged foursome, tanned and already pretty well lubricated, pushed the furniture around to suit themselves.

They summoned Bonita from behind the bar, ordered a

round of margaritas a little too loudly, and laughed continually until their drinks arrived.

Rather than stress over their noisy intrusion, Vanessa smiled and turned toward the beach. From time to time, she noticed Shiloh glancing at her, and although she didn't want him to, he caught her looking, winked, and flashed that magnificent smile. She chuckled under her breath at his obviousness and felt herself blush like a school girl.

Her drink drained, she slid off the stool a little unsteadily and walked to the beach. She pulled off her sandals, stepped onto the sand and gingerly sat in a hammock.

Swaying slightly, she listened to the chattering voices behind her and was lulled by the rustling palm fronds above her head. She sniffed the air, smelling a curious mix of coconut oil, a fragrant jasmine-like flower she didn't recognize, and the sea. Within a few minutes, she dozed off, stirring only when she felt someone's presence.

At first she thought she was dreaming and kept her eyes closed, letting the deliciousness of the total serenity wash over her, before she realized there really was someone standing nearby.

Reluctantly opening her eyes, she found Shiloh sitting cross-legged on the sand next to the hammock, a drink in each hand.

"I didn't mean to alarm you. I thought you might be down by the water, and instead I found you here. You looked so peaceful, I didn't have the heart to wake you."

"My God, how long have you been sitting there?"

He smiled, a little less dazzling this time, and spoke in a

quiet voice, "Not long, a few minutes. Oh, here—" he handed her a glass— "I made you a special drink."

A little unnerved by his stealthy approach, she gently nudged it aside and reached for the one in his other hand.

He smiled knowingly, didn't say a word, and handed her the glass. He clicked her drink with his and then took a swallow.

"What do you think?"

She brought it to her lips, touched the rim with her tongue to taste it, and then took a sip.

"What is this?"

"I call it the Shiloh Sling. Like a Singapore sling, only I use rum instead of gin.

"Whoa, no wonder I conked out. Rum can be deadly. I better lay off."

"No problem. The night is young, the breeze is warm, you are beautiful, and I am finished working for the evening."

She swung her legs out of the hammock and let them dangle just above the sand, stretching her arms out to grasp the webbing and steady herself before touching down with her feet.

Attempting to stand, unsteady in the swinging sofa, and tipsy from all the booze she had consumed, she fell against him, knocking him to the sand, but he held his drink aloft and not a drop spilled.

Laughing without a hint of embarrassment, she tried to get up, lost her balance and found herself atop him, her drink overturned in the sand. Shiloh squirmed to get out from beneath her, reached under her arms and hoisted her to her feet. Then he held her by the shoulders, turned her so she was facing him, and leaned in and kissed her.

"H-h-hold on, Cowboy," she said. "I'm not *that* drunk. What's the matter—no other single women in Belize at the moment?"

She was inches from his face, and in the fading light could still see his remarkably handsome features. Suddenly she was overcome with the urge to return his advance, and did, with a long, slow, searing kiss.

His hands cupped her face and stayed above her neck, but she was so engrossed in tasting a man's lips for the first time in more than a year, she didn't notice. She released the pressure on his mouth and stepped back.

Shiloh stared at her for a moment and then asked, "What do you mean, 'cowboy'?"

Vanessa laughed. "Just an expression."

He looked confused and she leaned in again, kissed him once more, took his hands and whispered in his ear, "The night is young, the breeze is warm, and you. . .are beautif—" Then she slumped onto the sand; her night on the town and her risqué dalliance was over.

He scooped her up and laid her gently in the hammock, grabbed beach towels from a cabana, covered her with them, and left. She awoke a few hours later, disoriented at first, with no recollection of what had happened or how she'd gotten into the hammock.

By the time she returned to the inn and found a night clerk, it was too late to get a taxi, but the desk man took pity on her and drove her back to the house in a canopied golf cart.

She handed him twenty Belizean dollars, but he refused

to accept them, saying he was happy to be of service.

Waking in the morning with a hangover, she lay low all day, drank copious amounts of water to flush her system, ate a light conch salad with some iced tea, and read. At dusk, the setting sun and lusty air got her thinking of the night before, and she wondered for the tenth time that day if anything had happened with Shiloh. She remembered kissing him, but that was the last she could recall.

She was embarrassed to go back to the Turtle Inn for fear that something had taken place that she hoped hadn't, but then, on the other hand, she wanted to have had a romantic liaison with the handsome stranger. If only she could remember. She had two more days, and one was a scheduled visit to the Mayan ruins.

CHAPTER SIXTEEN

Losing It All

P AOLO SPENT CONSIDERABLE TIME ruminating over Barbara's vanishing act or, at least, her indifference to the ringing phone. He thought of driving to her house and finding out for himself what was going on; he couldn't very well ask Hollingsworth if he knew where she was.

Charles was equally distraught at being stood-up by his ex and that she hadn't answered when he called.

His frustration turned to concern, and since he couldn't ask his vacationing daughter to do it, he decided to drive to Barbara's house and check on her.

Her car was in the driveway, the top down, the keys in the ignition; he felt the hood and found it was cold. He knocked quietly at first with no response, but as his annoyance grew he began to pound on the door. After a while, he walked around to the side of the house, but the blinds were closed.

He felt ridiculous; he had no key to get in and no real reason to be there or break down the door. He could always just hammer away at the window and doors, hoping she was only sleeping off another bender and would finally let him in.

He tried calling her from his cell but still got no response or voice mail intercept. Turning to walk away, he noticed neighbors watching from a window and waved to suggest his innocence of any wrongdoing; then he decided to ask if they had seen her, so he walked across the street.

Before he could ring the bell, a man opened the door a few inches. "Yes? Can I help you?"

"Hello. I'm—"

"Yes, I know who you are. What can I do for you?"

Only mildly surprised that the man—whom he didn't recall ever having met—knew who he was, Charles didn't offer a handshake. "I have been trying to reach Ms. Dearborn. Have you seen her recently?"

"Uh, no, I haven't, but that isn't surprising. She keeps to herself, and her newspapers often pile up outside. But then, it really isn't my business, is it?"

"No, I guess it isn't. Can you tell me when you saw her last?"

"Um, I don't know, maybe a couple days ago."

"Okay, thanks for your help."

The neighbor closed the door without another word. Charles crossed the man's lawn, shook his head, and muttered, "Jackass!"

He went back to Barbara's and knocked on the bedroom window; and finally he tried a side door and found it unlocked. He pushed it open and called out, "Barbara! Barbara, are you *home?*"

The kitchen smelled of stale coffee and decaying fruit. There were a few dishes in the sink, crumbs on the counter top, and a pint bottle of vodka lying on its side, the contents all but gone. He moved tentatively into the dining room and called out, a little hesitant and quieter this time, "Barbara?"

The television was on but not the sound.

He turned toward her bedroom, saw that the sheets and blanket were in a heap; one pillow was on the floor with a box of tissues lying next to it. He stood at the doorway and looked around before entering. The bathroom door was partially closed; he whispered, "Barbara. . . ?" before pushing it.

Blocked by something, the door didn't move very far. Charles felt his stomach churn and his heart accelerate. His knees buckled when he peered around the door and saw her crumpled, naked body wedged between it and the tub. He called to her again loudly, hoping she was only in a stupor.

"Barbara! Barbara, wake *up!*"

He knelt to touch her; she was ice cold. Then he saw the orange container and pills scattered on the tile floor next to her.

"Oh, Jesus! Oh, God, please. . . ." With some effort he was able to push the door and squeeze inside. Kneeling down he put his ear to her chest but heard no heartbeat. He took the container in his hand and tried to read the label, reached for his glasses, placed them on his nose and squinted at the writing. *Lexapro.*

He drew his fingers over her cold, dry lips; her eyes were wide open, staring blankly; her skin had a slight blue tinge. He sat there for several minutes before reaching for her robe behind the door; he spread it across her body and over her face and then went to the kitchen and dialed 911.

Two squad cars and an EMR ambulance, lights flashing and sirens wailing, arrived within six minutes of the call. A man in his forties, and a younger woman, both in tan uniforms and carrying medical apparatus, ran up the walkway.

Charles barely made it to the door; his legs were wobbly, his face streaked with tears, his lower lip trembling. The two responders pushed passed him, asking, "Where's the injured party?"

Charles had a momentary start.

"Uh, I...she's in the bathroom. But I think she's dead."

He pointed to the bedroom door. The paramedics followed his gaze and rushed to the other room, a policeman right behind them, as Charles sagged onto the sofa.

Minutes ticked by with sounds of attempted resuscitation coming from the bedroom.

One of the men reappeared. "You're Charles Hollingsworth, right?"

Charles glanced up, not sure how the fellow knew who he was.

"Yes. But how ... ?"

"I'm an artist. I've been to your gallery a few times. I'm afraid you're right, Mr. Hollingsworth...the woman...someone you know?"

"She was my wife. Is she ... ?"

"I'm terribly sorry, Mr. Hollingsworth. There's no sign of—I think she's been gone for several days, but the coroner's office will determine that."

"Coroner? Why. . .why can't I just have. . .the funeral home—"

"Routine, sir."

While his partner called it in, the policemen started to ask Charles questions about when he'd found Barbara's body, whether he had touched anything, the last time he'd seen her alive, and other things, one after the other, until a car pulled up outside. The newest arrival was a detective, and he, like the others, knew who Charles was. When he saw him on the sofa, walked over and patted him on the shoulder. "I'm sorry, Charles, What happened?"

"I'm not sure. I...do I need a lawyer?"

"I don't know. Do you think you do?"

"Edward, you know me. I might be a hard nose at times, but I didn't do this." He started to cry again.

Detective Edward Faulkner, a third cousin one part removed from the author William Faulkner, and quick to mention it when being introduced, took a breath. "Okay, okay, try to stay calm. I'll be right back."

Faulkner went into the bathroom and studied the scene, knelt, and lifted the robe covering Barbara's body; he sucked in air through his clenched teeth when he viewed her, covered her again, and walked back to where Charles was sipping a glass of water. "What can you tell me?"

Charles took a deep breath, ran a hand through his hair, and exhaled.

"I hadn't heard from her for days. We were supposed to meet for lunch, and she didn't show up. I wasn't too concerned— she does that sometimes. . . . Anyway, I tried calling several times, but got no answer and finally decided to come over and see if she was all right."

Faulkner slid the notepad he was holding into his pocket. "Maybe we better hold this 'til later."

"Am I a suspect?"

"No, Charles, at least not for now." Suddenly the detective's demeanor became all professional, friendship cast aside. "Charles, I'd like you to go sit in my car while I finish up here. You okay with that?"

"I'd rather go home, thank you. I really don't feel too well."

"Are you able to drive? Or do you want one of the officers to take you?"

"I can make it. It isn't all that far."

"Okay, but wait here for a while until I can let you go."

Charles stared at him incredulously. "Ed, what the hell are you talking about? This was my *wife,* for god's sake. She's *dead,* damn it. I don't know if it was an accident or she did it to herself. But. . .Jesus, Ed!"

"Okay. Fine. Go on home. I'll stop by later to see how you're doing. Does Vanessa know?"

"No. She's on holiday."

"You oughta give her a call. To let her know, I mean. When is she due back?"

He shrugged. "I think day after tomorrow. I can't recall."

Faulkner nodded, took out his pad again, scribbled something, then said, "Listen to me. You might still have to come in for questioning, so just pull yourself together if you do."

Charles lowered his head and shook it slowly from side to side. "Oh, God, Barbara. Why? What the hell did you do?"

Faulkner squeezed his shoulder again, turned, and headed back to the body; then he stopped and looked at Charles. "Go on. Get outta here."

Charles took a step forward. "I want to see her one more time."

"I don't think that's a good idea, Charles. Just leave."

"But what about—"

"Don't worry about anything. We'll tape it off and put an officer on duty. Is there something else you want to tell me?"

Charles shook his head and walked to the door in a daze. When he emerged into the sunlight, he glanced across the street and saw the neighbor he'd talked to earlier, standing on his doorstep with a drink in his hand, his wife behind him. Charles averted their inquisitive eyes, got into his Bentley, and drove away.

As he turned onto the main street, Paolo Rinaldi's bright red roadster with the artist behind the wheel drove past.

A still-dazed Charles didn't notice him, but the Genoan didn't miss the elite British automobile and sped up as it drove by. As the artist drew closer to Barbara's house and saw the police cars, his heart sank, and he stopped in the middle of the roadway just as the assistant coroner's car turned onto the street from the opposite end.

Paolo's eyes were wild with fear, his heart racing, his hands sweaty, his lips quavering. He made a U-turn and hurried back to his studio.

CHARLES ROARED UP HIS DRIVE, slammed on the brake, jumped out, and raced into the house. He made a beeline for the living room, threw open the cabinet door, grabbed a bottle of Macallan's 18, and poured some into a glass. He didn't bother to add ice or water. He sat on the sofa, threw the drink back, and drained it.

He put the tumbler on the table and rocked back and forth with an image of Barbara's lifeless body on the tile floor flashing in his mind, the scattered pills and the booze.

The goddamn booze, he thought. How many people destroyed by booze? How much beauty, how much talent wasted?

He'd pondered that thought throughout his unsettling love for Barbara. All of it flooded back in waves of despair while a concerned Fiona stood in the doorway, her hands clasped as if in prayer.

"Is there trouble, Mr. Hollingsworth?"

Charles took his hands from his face; his eyes rimmed in red, and haltingly replied, "Barbara is. . .Miss Dearborn is dead."

Fiona clutched at her heart. "What happened?"

Charles blinked several times, trying to be calm, but he couldn't hold it together. Fiona, never having seen her employer in such a state, was unsure of what to do. "Can I get you something? Some water?"

He squeezed his eyelids with his fingers and wiped at them with the back of his hand. "I'm sorry. It's just that. . .I can't believe. . . ."

She went for water and brought it to him in his study, where she found him searching frantically for Vanessa's phone number.

She set down the glass on the desk; an all encompassing sadness had stooped her shoulders; her face was crestfallen.

She had been there several times in the past to clean Barbara up before Charles got home and took pity on her rather than condemning her abject wastefulness.

Now, Charles himself seemed to have aged in a matter of minutes, his complexion sallow, dried saliva in the corners of his mouth, hands trembling as if riddled with Parkinson's.

Fiona stood by the desk, waiting for him to ask for assistance—something, anything. He absentmindedly moved things from one spot to another, lifting paperwork, shuffling files, without seeming to know what he was doing or even aware of Fiona's presence. He fell back into his chair, exhaled loudly out of exasperation, and finally looked at his housekeeper. "Thank you, Fiona. That'll be all. I can't discuss it now."

"I understand, sir. I will be in the kitchen if you need me."

He took a few swallows from the glass, inhaled deeply, moved his head from side to side, and arched his back, which had steadily stiffened with tension since he got home.

In her tropical paradise, Vanessa had risen early to meet the jeep tour heading to the Mayan ruins. The day turned out to be arduous, hot, humid, and rampant with insects, but still utterly fascinating and fun.

Returning to her rental before the sun went down, she had just stepped out of the shower, thrown on a pair of shorts and a T-shirt, and was standing barefoot, drying her hair, when the telephone startled her enough to make her scream.

It was the first time it had rung while she was staying there, and she lifted the receiver tentatively.

"Hello?"

"Oh, thank God. I wasn't sure if you'd pick up."

"*Dad?* What's the matter? Why are you calling? I hope this isn't about work, because—"

"Barbara's dead."

Momentarily dumbstruck, her knees buckled. She reached behind her to grab for the bed and crumpled to the floor.

"Vanessa, are you there?"

A sob caught in her throat. She felt faint and tried to speak, but nothing came out.

"Vanessa. Talk to me."

She grasped at a handful of hair and combed through it with her fingers several times before uttering, "Oh, God, Daddy, when? What happened?"

"I found her in the. . .she might have overdosed on pills. I don't know for sure."

"I'll get a plane out tomorrow."

He glanced at the itinerary Madeleine had given him.

"You're due back day after tomorrow. Just stay until then. There isn't much you can do here anyway."

"But, Dad, you need me there. I—"

"Don't worry about it. I just wanted you to know."

Vanessa was hunched on the floor, her head almost between her legs, feeling very sick.

A lengthy silence followed, the two of them alone in their thoughts but connected across the miles, taking an uncommon comfort in knowing they were still family, linked to Barbara.

"Dad, can you tell me more?"

He took a deep breath, calmed a bit, and slowly started to describe his experience.

"I hadn't spoken to her since. . .we were supposed to meet

for lunch. I tried calling and didn't get any answer, so I finally decided to go to her house. . .and that's when I found her."

"Dad, that's awful. Where. . . ?"

"I found her in the bathroom. An empty pill bottle, booze— just like you'd imagine."

"Dad, I am so, so sorry."

Another minute passed in silence before she said, "I'll try to get home tomorrow, but if I can't, I'll be there the day after. I wish I were with you now."

"I know. I know. There's still a lot to do. Her body is at the coroner's office, and there'll be an autopsy and an inquiry . . . ."

"Why do they have to. . . ?"

"They need to determine cause of death, to rule out anything suspicious. I don't know if they found a suicide note or what."

"Do *you* think she killed herself? I mean *intentionally?*"

"I don't know, I don't know. It wouldn't surprise me. She's tried before."

She let him ramble for a few more minutes, realizing he was more distraught then she would have expected.

When they said goodbye, she put the phone down and lay on the floor, overtaken by a deep sadness.

With only one flight to Albuquerque a day, getting a plane out of Belize on short notice was almost impossible, so she had to stick with her original schedule. The wait was agonizing. By the time she reached Santa Fe, all the benefits of her days on the beach, and change of scene, were gone.

CHAPTER SEVENTEEN

Case Closed

Cardiac arrest with possible renal failure brought on by a mega dosage of escitalopram oxcalate anti-depressant, on the order of 100 mg ingested. Approximately ten times the recommended amount. All that in conjunction with a BAC level of .30..."

So read the toxicology report indicating the cause of Barbara's death.

It took some fancy foot work, but the tragic occurrence was finally ruled as an accidental suicide, albeit pending further investigation. Charles was also successful at keeping the media in check, and the newspaper listed the death as an "unintentional overdose" of prescription drugs. Three weeks after the body was released for cremation, Charles held a memorial service. Paolo didn't attend.

One late afternoon a few weeks before the Rinaldi exhibition was scheduled, Celeste Silverman, a longtime friend and confidante of Barbara, strode into the gallery. Charles greeted her, and after her expressions of condolence, she took him by the arm.

"May I have a word with you. . .in private?"

"Certainly. Come into my office."

Thinking the attractive, fifty-something divorcée might be hitting on him, he entertained the idea of a brief liaison but shrugged it off as being inappropriate.

She held his arm until he closed the door, offered her a seat on the sofa, and went to sit behind his desk. "What's on your mind? Did you want to talk about Barb?"

"In a manner of speaking. Charles, you know that Barb and I were good friends. Perhaps I was her only *real* friend in Santa Fe. She confided in me. You know I never judged her. I just. . .just—" She stifled a sob, composed herself, and continued, "I just loved her. She was so feisty."

His eyebrows went up at the description, and then he smiled and nodded. "I suppose that's one way of looking at it."

Celeste raised her hand to keep him from saying anything more. He cleared his throat and leaned back, bemused but curious.

"Charles, are you aware that she was sleeping with Paolo Rinaldi?"

It took a moment to sink in, but Celeste knew from the look on his face that he had been caught completely off guard.

". . .Why—uh, why are you telling me this? Why *now?* Besides, we were divorced. She could sleep with whomever she chose. . . . As can I."

Based on what Barbara had told her, Celeste assumed the information would cut him deeply, and might even affect his relationship with Paolo, whom she found attractive but disingenuous. So telling Charles about Paolo was her way of honoring Barbara's memory, punishing both men for whatever pain she thought they had inflicted on her friend.

She glanced around the office, searching for a photograph of her, some token of his lost love for her, a tribute of some kind. But there was none. She slid her hand along the sofa cushion, feeling the heavy silk, letting the moment sink in, watching Charles for a glimmer of anguish. But he showed little, other than an almost imperceptible tightening of his jaw, which she missed.

The ticking of the ornate mantle clock was the only sound in the room. A few moments passed before he rose up from behind the desk. "Is there anything else?"

Incredulous at his low-key reaction, she slowly shook her head and got up. "You're a strange man, Charles. I thought you'd be more upset."

"No, Celeste, but I *am* saddened by her death. She lived on the edge with all that drinking, and, well. . .mixing it with drugs? As hard as it is to accept, it was only a matter of time."

He didn't see her out and spent the next half-hour contemplating what, if anything, he wanted to do with the information.

PAOLO PASSED HIS TIME getting ready for his one-man show, and when he wasn't painting, he raced around the mountain roads in his red Alpha Romeo. He made no attempt to call Charles and, while the silence troubled the gallery owner, he welcomed not having to deal with Paolo until he was ready to do so on his own terms. A few days after talking to Celeste, he picked up the phone. "Paolo, it's Charles Hollingsworth.

We need to talk."

"*Ah, buon giorno, singori.* You want to see the progress I have made, yes?"

"No, not quite."

"Then what can I do for you?"

"I'd like you to come to the gallery tomorrow afternoon. At one o'clock?"

"*Si, si.* I will be there. Uh. . .I was sorry to hear about . . .about your former wife."

"Thank you, I know we all miss her."

There was an eerie silence on the other end of the line. Charles waited another few seconds and then said, "Tomorrow, Paolo."

He hung up before another word was spoken.

ON SCHEDULE, PAOLO BRAKED his sports car, pulled into a space in front of the gallery, and climbed out wearing sandals, khaki slacks, and a pale blue Lacoste knit shirt. His hair was slicked back, a pair of sunglasses resting on top of his head. Jauntily entering the gallery, he greeted Dennis and Madeleine with a cheery "Ciao!" and kissed Vanessa's hand.

Not knowing Rinaldi had been summoned by her father, she was dismayed and felt left out yet again. She shook her head and turned on her heels. "I'll tell him you're here."

She stopped short of entering Charles' office and called to him, "Your one o'clock is here, Mr. Hollingsworth."

The sarcasm went unnoticed.

"Send him in, please."

"What the hell's going on here, Dad?"

"I'll explain it later."

"Shouldn't I sit in?"

"No. I'd rather have this discussion in private."

"Oh, I see—another deal that I should be part of, but I'm not?"

"Vanessa, not now! I said I'll explain later."

"That's it," she said just loud enough for him to hear. "I'm done!" Then she did an about face and headed into the gallery with Charles calling after her.

"What does that mean?"

"I'll explain it later," she mockingly called over her shoulder.

She rushed past Paolo, saying, "His eminence will see you now."

The two assistants eyed each other and then watched Vanessa enter the street and disappear up Canyon Road without looking back. Paolo shrugged it off and went to see Charles.

When he appeared in the doorway, Charles motioned with his chin toward a seat on the opposite side of his desk.

"Good to see you, *padrone*," offered the artist. "I was sorry to hear of your loss."

Charles nodded but didn't say thank you, and handed the artist a single sheet of paper. Paolo glanced at it and saw only one paragraph below the gallery letterhead. The final sentence caught his complete attention, ". . .dissolution of said agreement within thirty days of receipt of this document."

Charles had already signed his name above the space for Paolo's signature. His demeanor was perfunctory.

"I am handing this to you personally to avoid any possible argument that you never received it, but I will also follow legal procedure and send it by courier and have you sign for it . . . unless, of course, you want to sign it now?"

Paolo looked again at the document. "But why, Carlo? Why do you do this? I have been painting for weeks for our show. What is wrong?"

"I am no longer interested in associating with you or exhibiting your work. That's why."

The thought that it had anything to do with Barbara hadn't entered the Genoan's mind. Charles studied his face, looking for a glimmer of comprehension, some indication that he thought Charles might know about the relationship with Barbara. He held his Mont Blanc fountain pen toward Paolo.

"Here, you can sign this now and make it easier for both of us."

Rinaldi was immobile, shocked by the sudden turn of events, unsure of its ramifications. Then, in an instant, it occurred to him. "Ah. I see. It is because of Barbara."

Charles responded wryly, "What do you mean? What does my former wife have to do with you?"

Paolo nervously tapped two fingers against his mouth and narrowed his eyes, scrutinizing Charles, unsure how to reply. Hollingsworth looked out the window, sniffed at the Alpha Romeo, and thought of Barbara next to Paolo in that car. How many times? he wondered. How long had they been seeing one another, sleeping together? He slid his chair back from the desk and stood up.

"Well. . .take the document with you, sign it later then, and send it back. You can arrange to pick up your paintings. Our agreement is terminated thirty days from today. We're done here."

Paolo was aghast, his lips parted in disbelief. He scanned the room, looking for some clue, anything to explain the about-face. He took the sheet, seized the pen, scrawled his name, and set the pen and paper on the desk.

He held his hand out to Charles, but Hollingsworth didn't take it. "Sorry it didn't work out for you, Paolo. I'm sure you'll find someone else. . .uh, another gallery."

The artist brought his hand down and walked out of the Hollingsworth Gallery of Fine Art.

VANESSA CROSSED CANYON ROAD and turned onto Delgado, heading to number two-twelve. Yarbrough was with a customer, so she pretended to look at the work on the walls until she was able to catch his attention.

Bill spotted her, nodded, and went back to his conversation. ". . .Very perceptive," he was saying.

"How is it you are so knowledgeable about the German Expressionists?"

The man was much shorter than Bill, slight of stature, and wore white linen trousers topped by a tight fitting black tee-shirt; he had a little leather pouch in his left hand. She watched but tried not to be conspicuous. The man shifted his position, touched Bill's forearm, and replied, "I've always found some of them a bit, um, dark and deviant, but oh, so very . . .fascinating."

Yarbrough agreed, a tiny knowing smile in the corner of

his mouth. "Alright then, Mr. Weil, I will leave you alone with these for a few minutes. No rush. Take your time."

The photos Weil contemplated were original prints from Bill Owens' "Suburbia" series, a 1970s photo journey about the pursuit of the American dream.

Bill ambled over. "Hi, girlfriend. Do you need to talk to me?"

"Boy, do I!"

"This sale shouldn't take too long. You want to wait?"

"I'll sit across the street until he leaves."

He sashayed back to the client while Vanessa found a bench in the shade of a large oak. It was twenty minutes before Yarbrough and Weil appeared in the gallery doorway.

"Okay," she heard Bill say, "cocktails at the Kiva Café at five. See you then. And thank you—I know you'll enjoy these."

The diminutive man made his way to a black Mercedes, put the paper-wrapped package into the trunk, and slid into the front seat and drove off. Hoisting herself up, she crossed the street.

Bill was standing, with his arms folded, in front of the blank spots on the wall where the photos had been. "Well, my dear lady, do tell!"

Stressed and feeling anxious, Vanessa took hold of his arm and led him to a bench.

"Can we sit down? I want to ask you something."

CHAPTER EIGHTEEN

Crossroads

MARTIN SAT IN A PEW opposite the confessionals. Directly across from him, in the La Conquistadora, Our Lady of Peace chapel, he could see a robust woman, a shawl covering her head, lighting a votive candle, one of the dozens already flickering near the altar. She crossed herself several times and backed away. Passing Martin without looking at him, she stopped, turned toward the main altar, genuflected, and crossed herself again before heading out into the afternoon sun.

His hands, clasped in prayer, resting atop the shiny turned edge of the bench in front of him, Martin leaned forward and began reciting, "Hail, Mary...."

When he had completed the verse, he prayed in silence. Muffled noise from the apse echoed off the walls, but he was already too deep in prayer to notice. After awhile, not sure of how much time had passed, he heard a door open and saw Father Dominick enter. When the priest noticed Martin, he waited a few minutes before approaching.

"Hello, Martin, my son, are you well?"

"Yes, F-Father. I am."

"And your family? They are well, too?"

"Yes."

"Good. That is good. Are you here to seek guidance, my son?"

Martin was hesitant to speak. The priest studied him. "May I sit next to you, Martin?"

They sat in silence for several minutes, with their hands resting on the pew in front of them; there was a faint smell of burning wax in the air mingled with remnants of the incense used at early morning mass.

Father Dominick—a man in his late sixties, tall and thin, with a full head of silver hair—knew the Gomez family. He had said a prayer for Martin's mother at a mass after she died. He had enrolled Martin in the church student art group when Martin was in the sixth grade. And he had pressed to get him an art school scholarship.

After several more minutes, he rose and was about to say good-bye when Martin blurted out, "F-Father D-D-Dominick, I need to ask for s-something."

The priest sat down again.

"What is it, my son? Are you in some kind of trouble?"

Martin shook his head slowly, struggling to find the words.

"Take your time, Martin. . .it will come."

The young man took a few breaths and closed his eyes. "Father," he began, his stutter diminishing in the presence of the priest's stillness and the quiet of the church. "Father, I want to be a painter, b-but I need to work to make money. I can't do both—there is not enough t-time."

"Have you shown your paintings to anyone?"

"Only to my *tía*."

"I remember that you were a very good painter, Martin. I know it was God's gift to you. You must trust in Him. . . . Trust is here in Saint Francis; it is here, too, that risks for the Kingdom of God are taken, and where the gifts of everyone are called forth."

Martin turned to face the priest. "B-but how do I know I can make enough for my family?"

The priest contemplated this question. "Martin, have you done many paintings?"

"I have a lot, Padre."

"And do you think they are good?"

"I don't know, Father. I am not s-sure."

"Martin are you willing to show them to someone who will tell you?"

The young man thought about it, knowing he was at a crossroads, knowing he wanted to paint. . .more than anything else.

"Who, Father? Who would know?"

"Do you trust in Jesus, my son?"

"Yes, Father."

"Then have faith in Him now. . .to guide us both. I will find someone."

"Gracias, Padre."

The priest stood up and placed a hand on Martin's shoulder.

"*Vaya con dios, mi hijo.* Come next Monday at eleven. I will have an answer then."

LUPE APPEARED AT THE ENTRANCE to the study. "Doña Marta, Father Dominick is on the phone."

"Thank you, Lupe, I will take it in here."

She had always made certain she was readily available to the church and Father Dominick. The two often spent an hour in the church garden, speaking of secular things more than the spiritual. He was intelligent, kind, and genuinely concerned about his flock. She didn't hesitate to pick up the phone.

"Father Dominick. It is always a pleasure. You are well, I hope?"

"Yes, Doña Marta, and you?"

"Quite well, thank you. . . . Can I help you with something?"

"Actually, my dear, you can. And I am happy to say it is not for a donation this time. It is for a young man who has been a member of our church since he was baptized."

"I see. And what is it that I can do for him?"

"May I come by and see you to discuss it?"

"As it happens, Father, I will be at the Palace of the Governors this afternoon. Perhaps I could stop by and see you at the parish office?"

"That would be splendid. What time would suit you best?"

She glanced at a small clock on her desk, looked out toward the patio, and glimpsed the cloudless, brilliant blue sky.

"Late afternoon would be better. How is four o'clock?"

"I look forward to seeing you. I will explain everything at that time. *Hasta luego,* Doña Marta."

A highly influential woman, it was not unusual for her to receive requests for assistance: money, a recommendation, it could be almost anything. And for Marta Rodríguez y Encantada, no appeal went unheeded if she could do anything at all to help.

SHE AND FATHER DOMINICK SAT in the shade of a tree in the courtyard opposite the parish house and had iced tea while he explained Martin's background and conflict.

"He is such a goodhearted young man," he told her. "His affliction, a stutter that has been his burden since childhood, has never stopped him from serving his family, his church, and his—" he paused for a moment and then looked directly at her—"perhaps you have met him or seen him at the Kiva Café? He is a waiter there."

Marta thought for a moment. She knew Moira, of course, but rarely dined at the restaurant.

"I cannot recall. I am sure I would remember if I had met him, but it is of little importance either way. Tell me what it is that I can do."

"Martin," the priest continued, "has studied painting at the Institute and was in our school art program at Saint Francis when he was younger. He was very enthusiastic and seemed to be very talented."

Marta listened quietly, slowly nodding as the priest told her the story.

"I haven't seen his work in several years," he admitted, "so I don't know how he has progressed. But, then, I am not a good judge of art."

"Oh, Father, I seriously doubt that. I think you are far too modest. But tell me, where do I fit in?"

"Martin has come to a crossroads in his life. He told me he must give up painting because he has to support his family and has little time to pursue his art."

A few small birds pecking at the ground near them made fluttering sounds as they fought to seize each crumb before the other grabbed it. A tassel-eared Abert's squirrel suddenly darted out from under the bench and scattered the little winged creatures, catching both the priest's and Marta's attention. They chuckled at the mayhem before she returned to the conversation. "I'm still not sure what it is you want me to do, unless it is to look at his artwork and consider if he has the talent to make a living from it."

"Precisely, Doña Marta. That is exactly what I was hoping. I believe he will let you see it, even though no one else has, other than his family. He is very shy and doesn't tell anyone about his dream."

"Where can I see his work? Does he have a studio?"

"I will ask him on Monday and let you know. Everyone respects your knowledge, and you know so many people in the arts, it would be of great help.

"I know it is much to ask, but. . .if he has talent, perhaps you can point him in the right direction."

"Father Dominick, I will look at his art, but I would never tell him to stop working and chase a patently elusive dream. Many talented artists go unnoticed, or unfulfilled. It is as much a matter of luck—"

"And faith, my dear."

"Yes, and faith. But all the ability in the world cannot guarantee success. And if he must provide for his family, how could

I suggest he leave a paying job to go after something he might never achieve?"

"That is quite right. But let us begin by looking at his art first and then decide. Is that acceptable?"

"Yes, certainly. You arrange it, and I will do what I can."

He stood up, reached for her hand, and held it lightly, placing his other on top of it. "Bless you, Doña Marta. I knew I could count on you."

"*De nada, Padre. Y ahora, con su permiso?*"

Before leaving, she darted into the church, placed twenty dollars in the donation box, turned and crossed herself, and left. She walked to the corner of East Palace Avenue, where Douglas was waiting behind the wheel of the car. He got out and opened the door for her.

"Where to next, Doña Marta?"

"We're done for today, Douglas."

VANESSA INHALED DEEPLY, considered her words, and looked directly at Bill Yarbrough.

"Do you remember when I came back from New York, before going to work with my father?"

"Of course. It was only a couple years ago."

"Six, actually. Six years, and I have nothing to show for it. My dad is still too wrapped up in himself and...well, it doesn't matter. I've decided to quit."

Yarbrough raised his eyebrows. "Really? Well, can't say I'm surprised. But what—where do you plan to go?"

"That time six years ago," she started to explain, "before I started to work for my father, you asked me to work for you.

Are you still interested?"

"Oh, dear me, we *are* full of surprises, aren't we? Honey, that was a long time ago. I haven't thought about it since. I've had only one assistant in that time, and it was a disaster."

"I know this is sudden, but I'd only do it on an interim basis if you're willing. You know, a trial, of sorts. What do you think?"

"As an assistant? Oh, Vanessa, that just wouldn't do. You have so much talent. You could run this place better than me."

"I doubt that, but seriously, I need something. I love this place, you. . .the business, the work you show."

"When did you decide all this? I mean, to leave?"

"To be honest, Bill, I've been thinking about it for a good while. When I was in Belize, it started to make sense, and now— after Barbara's death, I thought he'd mellow out or take some time off. But he's worse than ever. I just want out. If it isn't here, then maybe I'll move down to Albuquerque or back to New York. It doesn't matter."

He scratched at his bald head and tugged at an earlobe while she waited. It seemed to her that he was struggling with the idea, and she sighed. "Bill, don't fret over it. I was just asking. I understand if you can't or don't want to."

"No, that's not it at all. You'd be an asset here. Let me think about it."

"Of course."

She looked around the gallery and thought how different it was from the Hollingsworth in every way imaginable. Not just the black-and-white photos versus the walls of color, but the decor, and, most of all, the demeanor. It felt calm, serious, yet playful, a total reflection of Bill.

"Have you told your father yet?"

"No." She frowned. "But I don't care anymore. When I decide what I'm doing and where I'll go, then I'll say something."

Bill could sense her uncertainty. "Do you have any place in mind? Other than the two-twelve, I mean?"

"Honestly, Bill, it's all very impetuous of me, so I need to regroup and give it some serious consideration."

He suddenly brightened. "Okay, how about this? You can work part-time here while you figure it out. That way we can test the waters, and you have a workplace to go to. I can only pay you twelve an hour, but with commission on what you sell."

She instinctively hugged him. "That would be perfect!"

"When do you want to start?"

She shrugged. "Dad's not gonna take this very well."

"You're not getting cold feet, are you?"

"No, I *have* to do this. I'm just not sure how he'll feel when he finds out that I'm working for you, but—" It suddenly occurred to her that Charles would probably think the envelope she had left on his desk with the Belize information had something to do with her decision, but she decided she'd just have to deal with it. "Bill, can I call you in a day or two, after I drop the bomb?"

"By all means. I wish you luck."

"You are such a good person, Bill. I mean it."

"Well, if I didn't feel the same about you, I wouldn't be doing this."

CHAPTER NINETEEN

Answered Prayers

KEITH DRAFTED A LIST of a dozen artists whose work he admired and who, as far as he knew, didn't have representation in the Southwest. He also went through unsolicited CDs of work. He chose six and invited the artists to send recent work for consideration; four responded.

It took a couple weeks to pull it together and go through each with Sonya; they chose two they thought would fit the gallery and hopefully fill the gap left by Rinaldi.

On Canyon Road and elsewhere, Keith and Moira were happily recognized as a couple and invited to attend events as such.

"When do you think we can include Deidre in our world?" She asked him one day.

"I've been wondering that myself. I wanted to be sure she's ready."

"Does she ask about us?"

"Yes."

"And what do you tell her?"

"That I like you very much, that you're fun, very pretty, and that she could meet you whenever she wanted to."

"That's a lot to live up to."

"But it's true, and I know she'll like you."

They decided to get together at one of Deirdre's favorite eateries, Chang's Palace.

MARTIN WASN'T SURE WHAT TO EXPECT when he got to the church the morning Father Dominick told him to return. He was wearing a pair of freshly pressed trousers and a white shirt. He smelled of Aqua Velva and his little sister Maya's strawberry scented shampoo.

After stopping to offer a prayer, he left a dollar in the donation box, crossed himself, and sat in the first pew.

At precisely eleven o'clock, a side door opened and Father Dominick entered, faced the altar, bowed his head, murmured briefly, and made the sign of the cross. Then he spotted Martin, came over, and sat down.

"Good morning, Father."

"Good morning, my son. How are things?"

"G-g-good, Father."

Father Dominick said with great excitement, "Martin, I have some wonderful news for you."

Martin's eyes widened, and he turned an expectant face toward the priest. His lips parted as if to speak, but nothing came out.

"Martin, do you know who Doña Marta Rodríguez y Encantada is?"

"I have heard of her. I d-d-don't *know* her."

"What have you heard?"

"That she is a very k-k-kind woman. That she is imp-por-tant."

"She is, my son. And do you know that she is also a patron of the arts and knows a great deal about it? She even owns an El Greco. Do you know El Greco?"

"Yes, Padre. I s-studied him in school."

"Well, Martin, Doña Marta has agreed to look at your work."

The priest smiled in anticipation, but it took Martin several seconds to process what was said before blurting, "I d-don't know if I'm r-ready."

Martin, you *are* ready. This has happened for a reason. You must take advantage of it. You said yourself that Doña Marta is kind. She will be honest and will help you decide. God has given you a gift, and you *must* use it for His glory, my son."

"But how will she see my paintings? I cannot bring them here."

"Would you be willing to let her come to your studio?"

"*Ai*, Padre, it is an old g-garage." He was clearly distressed and conflicted. "It is too far away!"

"Trust in the Lord, Martin, *La Doña* will come."

"When?"

"Whenever you say. But do not wait too long—it would be unfair to her. How soon do you think you can be ready?"

He didn't answer.

The priest slid out of the pew and stood up. "Think about it, my son. I will be back in a few minutes."

His shoes squeaked as he walked toward the altar. There

was the sound of a distant cough. A bright shaft of light entered the church as a door opened. And then it was silent.

Martin bowed his head, squeezed his eyelids with his fingers, and prayed for guidance.

CHARLES SEEMED UNFAZED by his dismissal of Paolo; it gave him a heightened sense of power and, in an odd way, some retribution for Barbara's death. It wasn't that he was jealous of them; it was more about his being unable to rein her in or keep her from harming herself. He knew he had never had control over her. But for Charles Hollingsworth, not having control was unacceptable, and being in charge wasn't the same thing as being in control; when it came to his ex-wife, he had neither. As for Keith Wheeler and the Twin Angels Gallery, Charles never gave it a second thought.

He scrolled through his address book and dialed a number.

"Hello, Anise?"

"Charles? Is it February already?"

He laughed at her sarcasm, cleared his throat, and launched into his pitch. "Anise, there've been some changes, and October has opened up. Can you be ready in time?"

"Charles, that's impossible! You know I was reluctant to commit to a February opening. There's no way in hell that I could have a show ready for October."

"What can I do to make you change your mind?"

"Do the paintings for me?"

"...How many *can* you have?"

While he waited for her reply, he patted his thigh for Brutus to jump up. The little dog's tail whipped back and forth like a high-speed pendulum, and was there in an instant. Charles scratched behind him behind the ear and gave Anise time to answer.

"I have five now," she said. "I could have one, maybe two, more. That's it."

"Not really enough for a one-woman show, is it?" he said.

"No, I guess not."

"Well, would you—"

"*No!* I would *not!*"

"How do you know what I was going to ask?"

"I will *not* do a two-person show, Charles, so you can just forget about it."

He wasn't surprised that she knew what he was thinking, but he was surprised that she was so adamant about it. Exasperated, he exhaled loudly and pushed Brutus off his lap.

"Just thought I'd ask. We'll keep it in February, then."

"...Tell me, Charles, what caused the change?"

He didn't want to explain, least of all to one of his artists.

"Just, uh...just a schedule conflict. Go back to work, Anise, I'll call you again in a few weeks."

When she had lung up, he reached for his Rolodex, rifled through the cards, and found one that he wanted. Not even aware she had left the gallery, he called out for Vanessa.

MARTIN RETREATED INTO PRAYER until Father Dominick returned.

"P-padre, I have m-m-made a decision."

"That's good, my son. No matter what, I am sure it is the

right one. Tell me, what have you decided?"

"I w-would like Doña Marta to see m-my paintings. Will she c-c-come to my house?"

"I will arrange it, Martin. You write the directions, and I will give them to her. Since you do not work on Mondays, I will ask her if she can come next week. Will you be able to do that?"

He nodded, clearly anxious but also resolved.

"Yes, Father. I will be ready."

"Martin, I think the Lord has been waiting for you to make this choice, and it is time for you to be recognized for your talent. I know you have not forsaken Jesus, and He has not forgotten you."

The priest rose, made the sign of the cross in front of Martin's face, clasped his hands and whispered, "*Vaya con dios, mi hijo.* Leave the directions at the Pastoral Center, and I will let you know as soon as I talk to *La Doña.*"

The young painter's mouth was dry, and he was beginning to perspire. He slid along the bench, got up, turned to the exit, dipped his fingers into the holy water receptacle, touched it to his forehead, crossed himself, and emerged into the harsh daylight, where he took a very deep breath, wiped the sweat from his brow, and brushed back his hair. His hands had stopped trembling, but he felt weak in the knees and sat down near the statue of Archbishop Lamy until he could gather his thoughts.

At home he waited until everyone was seated at the dinner table before he made his announcement. They said grace, passed the warm tortillas, and began filling their plates with *frijoles*. Verdad poured iced tea into everyone's glass. Russell kept looking up to study his brother's face and finally spoke out. "Brother, what is filling your head? You look as if . . ."

"I am s-showing my paintings!" Martin almost shouted.

The sisters looked at each other, wide-eyed, mouths open; Téja and Russell stared at him in disbelief. It was Téja who spoke first. "*Ai, joven!*" She clapped her hands together and looked to the ceiling, and murmured, "*Gracias a Dio. Diga me,* Martin. Tell me. Tell us. What has happened?"

His face was beaming with pride and at first the words didn't come. "Uh, uh, uh. . .Fa-Fa-Father Dominick is helping m-me. A very important l-lady in Santa Fe is coming to look at them."

They all cried out at the same time, "When?"

"M-Monday."

DOUGLAS DROVE DOÑA MARTA and Father Dominick to the Gomez house a little before noon. The road leading to the dwelling was dusty and kicked up a large plume behind the Jaguar as they approached the tiny modular home. The yard in front was only a few feet wide and lined with small rocks that were painted red, white, and blue. There were a few tomato plants and a small stone Madonna to one side of the doorway.

A worn set of temporary wooden stairs, resting on cinder blocks, led to the entrance. There was no sign of anyone in the house.

Douglas got out and walked to the door, but before he could knock, he heard a voice coming from the shed and saw Martin coming toward him with his hand over his brow, shading his eyes from the glare.

"H-hello?"

When he saw the young man, Father Dominick opened the car door, came around to open Marta's side, and called to him, "Martin, it's Father Dom and Doña Marta," and then, pointing toward the driver, added, "And this is Douglas."

CHARLES CALLED OUT AGAIN, "Vanessa!"

Having just come in from Bill's gallery, her heart was racing as she entered her father's office. She breathlessly said, "I'll be with you in a minute," turned, and went to her own office. Without waiting for his response, she closed the door, sat on the tiny sofa, took three deep breaths, and let them out slowly, until her pulse slowed.

She sat perfectly still with her hands facing palms up in her lap, her eyes closed. A few minutes passed before there was a knock on her door.

Still unaware that she had even left the gallery, Charles asked. "Vanessa, what's going on?"

"Come in, Dad."

He opened the door, saw the look on her face, and stopped cold.

"Are you okay? You look—"

"Dad, we have to talk."

"You're not upset about Paolo being here, are you?"

"It doesn't matter anymore, Dad."

"No, it doesn't, because I let him go."

She considered his words for a moment, shrugged, and, being as nonchalant as she could, said, "You haven't a clue, do you?"

He sat on the armrest.

"What does that mean. . . haven't a clue? About what?"

"Dad, I'm leaving."

"Again? You just got back."

"My point exactly! No, Dad, not for a few days. For good. I'm leaving the Hollingsworth. I just can't work like this anymore. I really thought you would give me my space, let me run the gallery, and that you'd ease off after Barbara. . . ."

"What does *that* have to do with it?"

"Nothing, Dad. . .nothing at all. I just thought you might see things differently after she died, but. . . ."

"Don't you want to know," he asked, "why I let him go."

"I can't *believe* you. Haven't you *heard* me?"

"Okay. What's on your mind, Vanessa? You want more authority? Is that it?"

"No, Dad. No. I don't want to *work* here anymore. I can't work *with* you. And I won't work *for* you. Now do you understand?"

His face reddened before he pushed himself off of the armrest and rose to his full height.

"Are you *insane?* What the hell has gotten into you? What do you mean, you're *leaving?* Vanessa, this is your job. You're my daughter. This gallery will be yours one day."

She scrunched her face as if she could taste the bile forming in her stomach, and at his choice of words, she woefully heaved a loud sigh. "It's done, Dad. I'll be out of here by the weekend. I'll fill in Madeleine and Dennis on where things stand, and if you want me to, I'll go over everything with you. Although I doubt there's anything I can share with you that you don't know, since I have so little knowledge of what goes on around here."

An ambulance racing down Paseo de Peralta, siren blaring, interrupted her. Charles turned toward the sound, but Vanessa just stared at him, not knowing what else to say, wishing she could make him understand how hard it was to love the father but so dislike the man.

He turned back toward her. "Look. Why don't you come up to the house tonight and have dinner, and we can discuss this."

"Dad, I can't. I can't do that. I'm sorry. You'll be fine. The gallery will do fine without me. It has *you*. I need to move on. Someday, maybe, someday you may understand. But then maybe you won't."

They looked into each other's eyes and held the gaze for a few moments before he said, "I love you, Vanessa. You're my only child, and I love you, and I am sorry you and I haven't ever really understood each other."

It seemed futile to her to prolong the exchange and try to say the things she felt. "I love you too, Dad. Let's give it a rest, okay? We can talk about it some other time. But it doesn't change my decision. I'm sorry, but I *am* leaving,"

She got up from the couch and walked to him. He rose, put his arms around her, and held her close. Then he kissed her on the forehead, let go, and stepped back. "I hope you'll reconsider, Vanessa. Please don't think I'm not upset about this. I'm not even sure why you are doing it, but...." He shrugged, patted her shoulder, and walked out.

CHAPTER TWENTY

Deliverance

KEITH AND DEIRDRE SAT IN A BOOTH on the far side of the restaurant opposite the entrance. "Dad, can I have egg roll?"

"They don't have egg rolls at a tea lunch, sweetie."

Her little girl face registered the mildest of disappointment and then she followed it with a barrage of questions about his "girlyfriend." When Moira joined them, Deirdre started the inquisition all over again.

"How do you know my daddy?"

"We work across the street from one another."

"Do you work in a art gallery?"

"No, Deirdre, I own a restaurant."

She thought about that for a moment and then asked, "Why aren't we eating there?"

Keith, holding back a laugh, shot a glance at Moira and answered, "Because it's her day off, and she wanted to eat somewhere that *you* like."

The youngster chewed a mouthful of spongy *sha shu bow,* swallowed, and said, "Thank you." Reflecting on it for a moment, she swung her spindly legs back and forth under the table and then asked, "What kind of restaurant is it?"

"It's a little fancy, a little Southwestern. . .would you like to come sometime?"

Deirdre eyed her plate and gave the invitation her utmost consideration, then looked at her father. "Would that be all right, Dad?"

Keith was about to respond when she turned to Moira. "By myself or with my dad?"

Moira and Keith both laughed, and she said, "Well, if you'd like to come by yourself. . . ."

"How would I *get* there?"

"How about we both go, Deirdre?" offered Keith, "That way, I can drive us."

"Okay, but can we go to the gallery after?"

"Absolutely!"

"When?"

"How about we get through *this* lunch first," he replied.

She made a face and went back to the bun on her plate, which she had chewed all around the outside without getting to the center. Moira shot a sideways glance at Keith and mouthed the words, "I *love* her!"

He reached for Moira's hand under the table and gave it a squeeze.

On the sidewalk afterwards, Moira crouched and spread out her arms. "How 'bout a hug?"

Deirdre looked at Keith for approval. He nodded, and she flew into Moira's arms and whispered into her ear, "I like you. Do you like me?"

Teary-eyed, Moira held the girl close to her a little longer than she expected to. Watching it, a thought ran through Keith's mind: *Kendra, is this okay? Please tell me it's okay.*

MARTA HELD OUT HER HAND to greet Martin, "How do you do? I am Marta Rodríguez y Encantada."

He shook it once, a little too hard, and took a step back. "M-M-Martin Go-Gomez. Thank you f-for coming to see my p-p-paintings."

The priest patted Martin on the shoulder.

"So, my son, this is a good day. People will soon know of Martin Gomez, artist!"

Martin blushed and motioned to the shed. "They are in the garage, b-b-but it is very dusty in there."

He hitched up his trousers and walked the few yards to the ramshackle wooden building where he had spent the morning tidying up, but the smell of turpentine, linseed oil, and varnish, and the mustiness of the shed, still assaulted the senses.

He had hung paintings from the beams, two on easels, the rest, sixteen of them, spread out against the walls, a few over-lapping because of the limited space.

Marta followed Father Dominick into the studio, but Douglas stayed behind when he saw how small the room was.

The display was stunning: a dazzling array of color and subject matter, mostly landscapes, but there were also portraits of family members and a few larger non-representational works.

Marta inhaled when she saw them and almost forgot to

let the breath out from the sheer surprise of what lay before her. In an instant, her trained eye saw a unique execution that suggested an assured hand had created them.

Wherever the brush stroke was broad, it had a consistent strength; when it was narrow, it exhibited deft control. She was struck by the young man's innate ability. She moved from one canvas to the next, pulled some aside to look at them, stepped back to view those mounted on easels, and examined those hanging from the beams. Martin stood perfectly still, afraid to speak or stir.

Father Dominick followed in Marta's footsteps, studying each work as soon as she moved to the next. His head moved from side to side, admiring the array, a tiny, satisfied smile in the corner of his mouth. Ten, maybe fifteen, minutes passed before Marta finally stopped and slowly, dramatically, turned toward the young artist. There was no measuring of words; she spoke clearly and directly. "Martin. These are wonderful. Every one of them is a work of great skill, and I have little doubt that you will find gallery representation."

Martin was frozen in place, unsure of what he just heard; he blinked twice before gripping the tabouret to steady himself.

"In fact," she continued, "I would like to buy these two—" she pointed to the easels— "if they are for sale."

He could barely speak. He'd never sold a painting and didn't know what to do or how much to ask. Marta saw his consternation and realized that she was talking to a gifted artist who had no idea how good he was. "Would you be willing," she asked, "to take a thousand dollars?"

Martin was flabbergasted. It was more money than he ever imagined his work was worth.

"For each," she added.

"I-I. . . ."

It was an overly generous offer, but *La Doña* was not being charitable—she believed his work would one day be worth many times that, and she said so. "Martin, I know that is probably more than you ever expected to make from your paintings, but I think what I have seen here is a very clear indication of your genius, and you should think of it as a shrewd investment on my part."

Feeling faint, Martin was reeling from the rapid turn of events, and his face was flush with excitement; his heart pounded against his sweat-soaked shirt.

The priest stood a few feet away, hands clasped in front of him, a proud, broad smile on his face, happy for Martin, happy for having thought to contact Doña Marta. When no one was looking, he raised his eyes to the rafters, quickly made the sign of the cross, and whispered, "Thank you, Father."

Martin shuffled his feet, shy and embarrassed. Unable to look at his benefactor, he murmured, "*Graciás*, Doña Marta."

"Then it's a deal?"

Martin nodded.

"Well, we must sit down and talk, Martin. I would like to help you. Would that be all right with you?"

Again he just nodded.

She smiled sweetly and said, "Perhaps we should go outside where there is more room."

It wasn't long after Paolo's abrupt dismissal from Hollingsworth Gallery of Fine Art that word spread throughout the community he was a free agent of sorts. Ironically, of the galleries that had space for his work or the clientele that could afford him, none were willing to offer the same arrangement he had with Charles. He had no one to turn to for advice.

Eventually, he called Keith.

"Hello, Paolo. I was expecting your call."

"Yes? Oh. . .I understand. You know about. . .?"

"Yes, of course I know. Everyone knows."

"Can we talk?"

"Paolo, I have little to say to you at this point."

After a few moments of silence, it was apparent that Rinaldi was uncertain how to proceed.

"Well, I guess that's it then," said Keith, "*Arrivederci.*"

"Wait!" Rinaldi implored. "Don't you want to know what happened? Why I left Hollingsworth?"

"Not really, Paolo. It doesn't matter. What matters to me is your disloyalty, and I could never, *never* work with someone who is disloyal."

Paolo pleaded, "It was business, nothing more."

"Yes, I suppose it was. Look, I wish you well, Paolo, but this is really a small community, remember that. Perhaps you should consider moving elsewhere." Keith didn't wait for a response. "I must go now—I have a customer in the gallery," he lied.

He felt a curious mix of emotions: hurt, anger, relief. Yet he also wondered if he was sabotaging himself by not reconsidering. He hadn't yet found a replacement for Paolo.

The very next day, he received a call, one that could not have been anticipated.

VANESSA ARRIVED AT THE GALLERY early on a Monday to clear out her desk and take her files and a few personal items from her office.

After moving everything into her car, she went back inside and wandered through the space, looking at the paintings, fingering the sculpture, running a hand over the back of her father's chair.

She sighed heavily and, after a few minutes, a tear trickled down her cheek. It was only when she was about to leave that she noticed the blinking red message light. At first she shrugged, deciding it wasn't her business anymore, but then she pushed the replay button and listened. "You have one message. Sunday, six p.m."

. . .*Hello, Charles?* She instantly recognized the Italian accent. *It is Paolo. I think maybe you know about Barbara and me and that is why you no want to represent me.* Vanessa's jaw dropped; her eyebrows rose in utter surprise. She could hear Paolo's nervous breathing. The disembodied voice continued, *I–I did not know you. . .that you still cared for her. For that, I am sorry. I would not have. . .been with her. I am . . .sorry.*

A few seconds of dead air followed, then the click of the phone. She stood in the gallery, unsure what to think, didn't erase it, and then exclaimed, "Whoa!"

MARTIN WAS RELUCTANT TO INVITE Doña Marta into his

house, so they stood outside for a few minutes and talked about his art. The area around the house, like many New Mexican communities in, on, or adjacent to pueblos, was desolate, with dilapidated dwellings, rusted cars, and old pickup trucks in their yards. The Gomez homestead was one of the better cared for.

"Martin," she finally said, "I think you have some important issues to think about before we can go any further. However, let me write you a check for the two paintings. I will take them with me, if it is all right with you."

Out of shyness, all he could do was nod and avert his new-found patron's eyes.

The priest understood Martin's discomfort and finally interceded. "Martin, my son, if it is agreeable, I will make arrangements with Doña Marta for another meeting, perhaps at the parish office, so we can discuss your future. Will that be okay with you?"

"Yes, I would like that very much. Thank you, Doña Marta. Thank you, Padre."

Not one of them seemed to notice that Martin hadn't stuttered for the past few minutes, not even he. On the drive back to Santa Fe, the priest and Marta spoke animatedly about what they had seen and about the extraordinary talent.

"Father, he is a truly gifted young man, but do you think he will make the transition? Is he ready to give up his job and focus on being a painter? Can he make that commitment without having some assurance?"

Douglas slowed the dark blue Jaguar XJ and turned onto the highway and headed toward Santa Fe. Father Dominick looked out the window and thought about what she had asked.

The afternoon sky was filling with high clouds north of the city, yet the light was still very bright and in marked contrast to the shadows on the distant mesas and cliffs.

The priest sighed. "I don't know. It will be a major change for him, and a very big risk. I'm not sure he has the confidence, but your remarks, your generosity, will go a long way to convince him. Tell me, Doña Marta, do you really think he can find a gallery to show his work, that he can make a living from it?"

Even in the back seat of her car, the doyenne's posture was exemplary. She sat with her hands resting in her lap, ankles crossed, back straight. "I have absolute confidence in what I saw today. But I have many questions for him before I can suggest a gallery. He will need to be honest with me, and most of all, with himself, before I can recommend him."

She gazed out the window for a few seconds before continuing. "The business of art," she finally said, "is as much about social politics as it is about the work. Many artists cannot deal with the pressure of deadlines and shows. Many of them lack the discipline and aren't comfortable selling their art, nor do they know how. The most successful understand how to charm the collectors, how to create an aura about themselves and their work."

She closed her eyes to collect her thoughts and then turned slightly to face the priest. "From what I have seen," she continued, "Martin is a very shy young man, unsure of his talent, and he has no idea of what it will take to be successful. But. . .and this is important—" she uncharacteristically held up one finger to emphasize her next comment— "it is clear that he has a passion for painting, and judging by what we saw back there, he seems as dedicated to it as any professional artist I know."

The priest knew that she, more than anyone in Santa Fe, could help Martin succeed. He sensed, too, that the only obstacle would be Martin Gomez.

CHAPTER TWENTY-ONE

Joy And Sorrow

AFTER HER FIRST DAY AT GALLERY 212, Vanessa understood that Bill's collection and billing system would require a paradigm shift in her thinking. Selling photography, even with the major players that Yarbrough represented, was very different from dealing in paintings and sculpture. Prices for recognized photographers' work were generally lower than the prices Hollingsworth Gallery received for its established artists.

Bill walked her through the subtleties with courtesy and patience. "I'm sure you already know most of this, but it will be good to review it," he told her, but then confessed, "My belief is that most any art reproduction, like *giclée* prints, for example, diminishes in value with the number of prints produced."

"I'm not a big fan of *giclée*," she said. "It's like buying a page from a magazine."

She knew she could never have admitted that to Charles. He made a lot of money from the sale of *giclées*, mostly from people who couldn't or wouldn't pay the thirty-or forty-thousand- dollar price tags for some of his mid-range artists. To less discerning patrons, buying art for a tenth the price seemed like a great investment. Because the artist "embellished" the *giclée* with a dab of paint and signed it, many buyers were satisfied to call it an original.

Hoping to learn as much as she could as quickly as possible, she peppered him with questions throughout the day.

"How many prints does a photographer make before destroying the negative?" Then after considering her inquiry, she added, "They *do* destroy the negative, right?"

"It depends on the photographer," he said, "or when the image was made, or the print process used. It's doubtful they'd destroy anything archival."

He expanded further on the production of multiple prints and voiced his own belief. "With etchings and lithographs, for example, editions of anything over fifty really have no business being called a *limited* edition, in my opinion. As for a photograph," he mused, "I like to think in terms of no more than ten prints from a negative, preferably processed by the photographer. Unfortunately, that's not always the case, particularly now, with digital being the norm."

"…How can you know for sure?"

"I try to get an accurate accounting, no matter what. But then, that's not always possible," he explained. "The artist might have died, or their estate might be in control. Anything can make it difficult to know exactly. It's one of the reasons I only deal in established photographers with a record of provenance. It's also why we can charge top dollar."

That he used the word "we" and not "I" was duly noted by

Vanessa, who was enjoying herself and Bill's willingness to share information. What a difference, she thought.

Bill spent several days reviewing billing procedure and discussing the nuances of the work on display.

Each night, he sent her home with dossiers on clients, and backgrounds on all the represented photographers. She was familiar with much of what he was telling her, but she soaked up everything else. Her third week in the gallery by herself, she sold a Sebastían Salgado for eighteen thousand dollars!

As for Charles, she had called him the day before she started at the 212.

"I didn't want you to hear this from anyone else," she started, "but I'm going to work at Gallery 212 beginning tomorrow."

"Well," he said sarcastically, "maybe it would have been better that I *did* hear it from someone else. I haven't seen you since you walked out."

"I'm sorry, Dad. I just need to give this a chance. I'm not able to talk to you about it because, if I were, I wouldn't have left in the first place."

He tried to absorb it.

"I promise you, Dad, I'll come for dinner next week, and we can talk."

"I'm not happy with this."

"I know you're not, but can't we just discuss this when I see you?"

"You're not giving me much of a choice."

Spending another second on the phone with him would have made her feel guilty; she ended it saying, "Dad, I have to go. We'll talk later. Bye."

She hung up the phone before he could say anything more. It was a small triumph.

BILL WAS ELATED WITH HER SALE of the Salgado—not that the Brazilian's work was a difficult to move, but because it had been in the gallery only a month. Contrary to normal business protocol and in order to show his appreciation, he cut Vanessa a commission check the same day.

She took him to lunch at the Kiva to celebrate. They drank a bottle of Trebbiano and were the last to leave, but not before Moira stopped by their table.

"What are you people up to?"

Bill, reaching for a chair said, "Please join us, Moira. We're celebrating Vanessa's first sale at the Two-Twelve. You know she and I are working together, right?"

"Yes, I'd heard that. . . ." Moira thought about it for a second and then asked, "Are you partners now?"

"No, no," Vanessa interjected. "Not at all, I work for Bill. I left The Hollingsworth a few weeks ago." She said it as if she were no relation to Charles. "But that's a long story."

Moira nodded knowingly. "The street is rife enough with rumor and innuendo, Vanessa—you know that as well as any of us. There's no need to explain. I'm sure you had a perfectly good reason."

SONYA ANSWERED THE PHONE on the second ring and then called out, "Keith, Marta Rodríguez is on the phone for you." He took the call without hesitation.

"Good afternoon, Doña Marta. What an unexpected pleasure. How have you been?"

"I am fine, Keith, thank you. I am hoping you can help me with something."

"I'd be delighted. What can I do?"

"I understand that Paolo Rinaldi and you have gone separate ways, and I wonder if you are seeking any new artists."

"As a matter of fact, we are. Do you know of someone?" Like most gallery owners in town, he trusted her judgment on virtually anything to do with the arts.

"Yes," she answered, "I do."

"Who?"

"I'd rather not say at the moment, but I would like to meet with you. Are you available tomorrow?"

He was curious about her need for secrecy, but didn't pursue it; tomorrow would be soon enough. "May I ask, Doña Marta, if you've spoken to anyone else about this?"

"No, Keith, I haven't."

"Why m . . .why the Twin Angels Gallery?"

"For several reasons. I trust you, and I know you are a compassionate human being and treat your artists with great respect. I think this person will need careful guidance, and I believe you can provide that."

"I am flattered, Doña Marta. Of course I will help if I can."

"I knew I could count on you. I will come to the gallery. Is three o'clock all right?"

He checked the appointment calendar. "Three's perfect. I look forward to seeing you and hearing more about this. Thank you for thinking of me."

"You were the first one that came to mind. I will see you tomorrow."

He hung up, mulled it over, wondering who the artist might be, and shrugged, happy that she had thought to call him before anyone else. He immediately told Sonya. "You have any idea who it could be?" he asked.

"Not a clue. I haven't heard about anyone leaving the fold, other than Paolo. I don't know of anyone new in town either. You?"

He shook his head, picked up a turquoise-and-silver paper weight atop a stack of color prints and absently leafed through them. "Anyone of interest in this pile?"

"No. Maybe one or two, but nothing special. I've looked through these a dozen times."

He shrugged again. "Okay. Well I guess we'll just have to wait until tomorrow. You want a coffee?" She said she did, and he headed for the door. "Be right back."

As soon as he was out of sight, she reached for the phone, hit a speed dial number. After two rings, a woman answered. "Good afternoon. Hollingsworth Fine Art."

VANESSA WAS POSITIVELY UPBEAT over the Salgado sale and elated with the way Bill treated her, convinced she had made the right decision leaving her father's gallery.

A week later, she sold a pair of Mapplethorpe prints, making it the best month the 212 had ever had. Bill bought her a bottle of *Crystal* to celebrate. "You are a gem," he told her. "I can't tell you how long it would take most people to catch on the way you have. And to make a sale so soon. . .outrageous!

Remind me to thank your father for being such a horse's ass."

She stifled a laugh. "Speaking of reminding," she said, "I promised him I'd let him know my plans."

Bill was thumbing through an edition of *Aperture* magazine and didn't look up but asked, "And what might those be?"

"He still thinks I'm here on a temporary basis, until he gives in or I give up. That's not going to happen, either way."

Bill closed the magazine and looked over the top of his glasses. "So what's there to tell him?"

"Just that I'm staying here and that I'm happy with my decision."

Bill approached and laid an avuncular hand on her shoulder, "What if…what if he *does* change his mind and makes you an offer worth taking?"

She hadn't considered it, knowing it was too out of character for Charles Hollingsworth to give in to anyone, not even his daughter. "There's about as much chance of that happening as you getting married."

"As a matter of fact—"

"As a matter of fact *what?*"

Bill actually blushed. He removed the glasses from his nose and let them dangle from the chain around his neck. "As a matter of fact," he repeated, "I think I'm in love."

"No! With whom?"

"Remember that adorable man who bought the Bill Owens images?"

"Mr. Weil? Really? Bill, that's—does he know?"

"Of course! We've been seeing each ever since."

"I thought he was from out of town."

"He rented a place here."

"Whoa! That's serious. Well, I'm thrilled for you."

He put his hands together, made a little motion with his head and brought one hand up to his cheek, his eyes brimming with joyful tears. "It's been so long since I've felt this way."

Vanessa could only nod, though, while she was happy for him, she felt it inappropriate to pry. He sighed, grinned sheepishly, and sighed again.

"Well, there you have it, then," he said as nonchalantly as he could muster.

A short silence followed, and then he straightened to his full height, pulled his glasses on, and swept back to his desk.

CHAPTER TWENTY-TWO

To Brilliance

SONYA WAS RELIEVED that Madeleine had picked up the phone instead of Dennis, because he'd probably blab it all over town.

"Maddy, it's Sonya. Got a question."

"Hi, Sunny. What's up?"

"I have to talk fast—Keith would be ticked off if he knew I was calling. Listen, do you know of any artists, other than Rinaldi, who are without representation right now?"

"Yeah, like thousands!"

"No, I mean locally. Anyone been showing their portfolio 'round?"

"Uh, not that I know of. Why?"

Sonya had her eyes trained on the street, watching for Keith. The Road was quiet except for a lone gray cat casually strolling along the sidewalk as if to torment the dogs in the neighborhood. Then she spotted her boss carrying two containers. "Oops, can't say right now. Gotta go. Keith's coming. I'll talk to you later."

She quickly put the phone down and focused on her Post-

It note-covered monitor.

Keith handed her a coffee container. "Got you a latte. . . and a chocolate macadamia brownie."

She smiled with one tiny dimple creasing her cheek, and her hazel eyes registered thanks, but she shook her head in mock disgust. "Thanks, but I could do without the calories."

"You're welcome."

He sank onto a chrome-and-brown leather director's chair, set his coffee on the edge of the desk, gently lifted the lid, brought the container to his lips, and blew on it between short sips.

He made a little motion towards her with the cup, "Here's to tomorrow. Let's hope whoever it is. . .will be brilliant."

"To brilliance," she said.

BUOYED BY SUCCESS, Vanessa called Charles to set things right or to at least let him know she was not returning to the Hollingsworth. She wanted to meet him at a restaurant to avoid a scene, but he insisted that she come for dinner at the house.

Sunday evenings had always been their attempt at a family dinner, even when she was a child. Things had changed when he was married to Barbara and she herself had moved to New York. Father and daughter tried to resurrect the tradition, if that was the word for it, when she returned to Santa Fe, but it had been sporadic.

Feeling light-hearted and happy when she first got into her car to drive to Tesuque, her mood changed as the house came into view. She pulled into the circular driveway, stopped the car, and waited until her breathing had slowed. Then she combed her hair, pinched at her cheeks, inhaled deeply, and got out.

She didn't use her key but rang the bell. Then, feeling odd about it, she tried the door, found it open, and walked in. "Hi, I'm here."

Fiona came out of the kitchen and greeted her.

"Hello, Miss Vanessa. You look beautiful as always. How have you been?"

"Fiona, so good to see you. I am doing great. How are you?"

The woman nodded several times, offered a tiny shrug in response, and smiled sweetly. Charles' voice boomed from the study. "In here, Vanessa."

There was a beaker of martinis sitting on the coffee table and a dish of pimento-stuffed olives alongside a plate of smoked salmon and dill canapés. He rose and kissed her on the forehead. "Don't you look lovely. Good to see you, sweetheart."

Well, he's in a good mood, she thought. He reached for the pitcher, his glass already half-drained. "How about a drink? Bombay Sapphire, two Spanish olives, no ice, right? Just like ol' times, eh?"

"I better not, Dad, I—"

"What do you mean? You have to have a drink with the ol' man. It's a Sunday night ritual. Or have you forgotten already?"

"Okay, but only a half." She said it with a barely audible sigh.

"That's the spirit." He poured it almost to the brim.

"Oops, sorry. Well, just drink what you can."

She took the glass with two hands so as not to spill any on the Persian rug. Holding it close to her lips, she gingerly sipped at it until she felt assured it wouldn't splash over the top, set the glass on a coaster, and took a seat on the couch.

Charles held his glass aloft. "To you, my darling, and to old times, the best of times."

As far as she could remember, the old times hadn't been all that good and certainly not the best, unless you went back to her childhood. She raised her glass anyway, gave him a little smile, and took another sip. Charles sat in a chair opposite her—a big, dark green, leather wing-back, the type often found in a men's club. He sat back and crossed his legs, sniffed, brought the glass to his lips, took a drink, and placed the glass on the side table.

"How are things at the Two-Twelve? Not as hectic as the Hollingsworth, I suppose."

"Not as frenetic, that's for sure."

"Have you sold anything yet?" He posed it with a touch of sarcasm.

Vanessa cringed, but let it slide. "Yes, as a matter of fact I've sold several."

"Well, well, well. I have no idea how much you make in commission, but I dare say it isn't close to what you would have made at Hollingsworth."

Exasperated, she chewed at her lower lip but didn't reply. Charles tipped his glass in her direction. "Well, congratulations. I can't say I'm surprised."

Vanessa leaned forward and touched a few familiar objects

on the coffee table, the large brightly colored hand-blown glass bowl, the silver cigarette box filled with foreign coins, the over-sized book about the paintings of David Hockney, the framed photo of Charles and herself at age twelve aboard a yacht in Porto Cervo, Sardinia. Her mother had taken it. She touched her finger to the image, remembering that day, letting a tiny sigh escape. Contrary to her promise not to drink that night, she took another sip of the martini without looking at her father.

During their dinner—which consisted of veal scaloppini, an arugula salad, and a bottle of *dolcetto d'Alba*—Charles chided her about leaving the gallery and "breaking his heart."

Vanessa refused to be drawn into it. "Dad, I need to do this for me. I have to be my own woman. You and the gallery will do just fine. Besides, I'm still on Canyon Road—it's not as if I moved *away*."

He stopped poking at the food, put the fork down, slowly wiped his mouth, and stared at her across the table. She averted her eyes while making tiny scraping noises on the Rosenthal china plate with her knife, until she slid a small piece of scaloppini between her lips and washed it down with a swallow of the Italian red. "Can we change the subject?"

He reached for his goblet, held it under his nose, swirled it around in the glass, and narrowed his eyes. "What would you like to talk about?"

She wondered what might be a safe topic, knowing that, if she asked about Anise's show or Paolo's exit, it would only lead to more snide commentary.

Charles fed a tiny piece of meat to Brutus, who had been

sitting on his lap all through dinner. The dog nipped at it, made a tiny chewing sound, hopped onto the floor, and trotted to his water bowl in the kitchen.

Following another awkward silence, Charles pushed away from the table and said, "Well, I guess we have little else to discuss other than art, huh? Too bad, really, we used to be such friends. Remember how I could make you laugh when you were a little girl?"

She nodded. "Yes, I do. I miss that. What happened to you, Dad?"

"What do you mean? Nothing happened. I'm still the same."

"No, Dad, you're not. After Mom died, you lost the laughter in your eyes. You became...I don't know, all about business."

She closed her eyes, trying to remember him from twenty years earlier, the man she worshiped, who could always make her giggle by tickling her, by making funny faces, by telling silly jokes. She missed that person and those days when there had been a family.

When she opened her eyes, Charles was gazing at her with such a sad expression that she leaned across and took hold of his hand. He squeezed her fingers and held them for a few seconds; he cleared his throat. "I guess a few things...." He didn't finish.

Fiona cleared the plates and brought a French coffee press to the table and a dish of amaretto cookies.

Charles took one of them, removed its colored tissue wrapping, held it between two fingers over one of the candles until it took the flame, and then let go and watched it float up toward the ceiling and evaporate into thin air. It was a little trick he used to amuse guests. Vanessa smiled, Charles winked, and their evening together suddenly felt better.

A DARK BLUE JAGUAR pulled up to the curb in front of the Twin Angels. Douglas opened the door, and Marta emerged onto the sidewalk. He popped the trunk, extracted a large brown paper-wrapped package, carried it to the entrance of the gallery, and rested it just inside the door. "Thank you, Douglas. Please pull around back and wait for me there. I won't be terribly long."

Not another car had come along while Douglas idled in front of the squat adobe building; it was a quiet day on Canyon Road. Douglas nodded, slipped behind the wheel, and trundled down the street.

Keith spotted her before she entered and met her at the door.

"Good afternoon, Marta. Thank you for coming. I'm eager to see what you've brought."

He motioned to the parcel. "Should I open this?"

She playfully replied, "Not just yet."

He chuckled, sat next to her on the sofa in his office, crossed his legs, and turned sideways to face her.

"Allow me to get right to the point," she said.

"By all means, please do. My anticipation has been unbearable."

"Keith, Father Dominick, at Saint Francis, was kind and thoughtful enough to introduce me to one of his flock—an undiscovered and *very* gifted painter. I have a feeling you will agree, and I promised the artist and Father Dominick that I would try to help."

He shifted his weight, barely able to contain himself, knowing that she never spoke flippantly about art. He knew too, that her opinion was more astute than that of most any art critic. "When I first saw the young man's work," she said with a touch of reverence, "I was stunned by its beauty and his innate ability. . .and I immediately purchased two canvases."

"Then he's a *local* artist? Has he shown anywhere here?"

"No, that's the fascinating part. He's quite. . .quite shy, and he has no idea how fine he is. The saddest part of it is that he has been working right under our noses all along." She looked directly into Keith's eyes, "Would you like to see what I have brought?"

Keith rose. "I can hardly wait! Now?"

"Please."

He glanced at Sonya in acknowledgment, lifted the package by the cord tied around it, and asked, "All right to cut the twine?"

"By all means, Keith. But before you do, I want you to know what is on my mind."

He gestured for her to continue.

"The young man is not untrained, but he is from a poor home and is largely responsible for his younger siblings. . . ." She fixed her eyes on Keith, who stood poised with scissors in hand. "Yes? Go on."

"No, it can wait. Open it."

Before he could remove the wrapping, the door chime rang, and he glanced toward the entrance to see a thin, weathered-looking man, perhaps in his thirties, enter the gallery. The fellow was wearing a wide-brim canvas sun hat with a rawhide string tying it to his chin. His khaki trousers were held up with a pair of dark green suspenders; his feet were encased in a pair of worn leather hiking boots. He had a large rucksack strapped to his back with a fold-up French easel attached to it.

A *plein* air painter, thought Keith; Sonya will take care of it. He turned to Marta, wondering if this was her painter. But she remained expressionless. "You're not expecting anyone, are you?" he asked.

"I assure you not."

He cut the cord and let it fall to the floor, then pulled at the tape to free the two canvases inside.

Her eyes were trained on him and his initial reaction. He reached behind the first painting to grasp the wooden stretcher to which it was tacked. He propped it against his desk. He reached for the other one, and, catching only a glimpse, his eyes widened. He stepped back, pressed himself against the far wall, and broke into a wide grin. "You've got to be kidding. These are by an *unknown artist?* He's never shown anywhere?"

"No. Not many people even know he paints."

"Okay, okay, who is it? What's his name?"

"You probably know him, or of him, but not as an artist."

"Really? How?"

"Two ways, actually. In fact, you may even have talked to him."

"Come on, tell me. Please!"

She was enjoying the little game. "First, tell me what you think."

He scrutinized them for a few minutes. Then he straightened up. "Marta, these are exceptional. . .in every way. His palette is exquisite. The work has a great dynamic. Does he have more like these? Where's his studio? Who is it? Can I meet him?"

By then, she was smiling triumphantly. "It is the work of Martin Gomez."

He looked perplexed, searching for the name in his memory bank, unsure of who the man was or if he *did* in fact know him. He shook his head almost imperceptibly, shrugged once, and beseeched her with his eyes.

"Your housekeeper?" she hinted.

He wondered what Téja had to do with it.

Finally, she exclaimed, "Martin is Téja's *nephew*. He works across the street. . .at Moira's!"

"Oh, my God!" He slapped his forehead. "*He's* the one she told me about."

"Moira *knows* about him?"

"Not exactly. . .she told me somebody working for her was a painter, but she hadn't seen his work and didn't know if he was any good. She didn't say who it was."

"I am so pleased you agree with me about his talent. He is a real find, don't you think? And there is no one on Canyon Road I would rather have represent him than you."

Keith returned to the paintings, peering at them through a tiny frame he formed with his two hands, studying them in sections. He was crouching in front of one and turned to face Marta. "When did he produce these?"

She explained Martin's background just as Father Dominick had told her, and described Go-Go's hesitation to take the leap of faith needed to paint full time.

"Marta, can you arrange a studio visit? I want to meet him right away."

"I will ask Father Dominick. I know he'll be very pleased, and I am certain he'll speak to Martin and advise him to see you."

"Thank you, Marta. I am very grateful for this opportunity. I assume he has other paintings like this?"

"Yes, but his work is so diverse—it is as if more than one artist created them."

"Marta, I haven't been this excited about an artist since .. .Paolo Rinaldi."

"Then I am pleased, and wish you both great success. I hope you can convince him to expose his work to the public. That is the main stumbling block."

She rose from the sofa and extended her hand. He grasped it with both of his. "I will hear from you, then?"

"From me or Father Dominick."

He re-wrapped the paintings and brought them to the rear doorway, where Marta was meeting Douglas.

"Thank you, again. Be well, Marta. *Vaya con dios.*"

"*Vaya con dios*, Keith."

Almost giddy from what he had just seen, he went into the gallery space, where Sonya was talking to the hiker.

"Keith," she said, "I'd like you to meet Karl Meisner. He's from Austria."

Keith shook his hand. "Welcome. I see you have an easel. Were you out painting?"

"*Ja, ja*, I *vas*. I visit America for three months."

"We don't usually accept unsolicited portfolios, but—well, you're here. Did you want to show us something? Do you have any of your work with you?"

"*Ja*, I have some in my bag." He nodded in Sonya's direction, "I showed them to this beautiful lady."

Karl opened the rucksack and removed several tiny canvases, none larger than a sheet of loose-leaf paper. Each depicted a landscape: Ghost Ranch, the Plaza in Santa Fe, Taos Gorge, Loretto Chapel, an early morning scene of Canyon Road. His style was unique, not typical *plein* air realism, but more hard-edge and graphic, with intense colors.

Keith tapped his fingers against his lips while looking at the work and glanced at Sonya to see her reaction.

"Tell me, Karl, are you represented anywhere?"

"Yes, I show at art gallery in Kitzbühel, and also in Amsterdam, but not in the United States."

"Are you hoping to?"

"Yes. It is my plan."

"And what is that, exactly?"

He lifted his hat and scratched at his scalp as if searching for an explanation. Then he let the hat fall back and rest against his shoulders, held by the chin strap.

He crouched to rummage through his rucksack and came up with a plastic-wrapped folder containing dozens of newspaper and magazine clips.

"These are. . .how do you say. . .? Uh, reviews? Please, you can look at them. My idea is to move to America, but I must have a gallery before I can do that. Are you interested? I have photos of more work in my bag."

"We might be, but I am about to see another artist's work, and frankly, while your work is good, it's quite *small* for our needs."

Karl offered a tiny smile, rose to his full, substantial height, and hitched up his trousers.

"These are just studies, sketches only. I use them for notes. I paint more big in my studio in Vienna."

"How big?"

He gestured with his arms. "Maybe one meter by two."

"Oh, that's good, large enough to command higher prices. Yes, I *am* interested in talking to you. Will you be in Santa Fe a while?"

The man looked dismayed by the question, pursed his lips in thought, wiped a hand across his mouth, and after a while replied, "I going to Vyaming tomorrow, but. . . ."

Sonya asked, "You mean Wyoming?"

"Yes, this place Vyaming. . .Jackson's Hold."

"You mean Jackson Hole? Yes, it is another good art town," she said.

Keith was clearly interested. "Can you stay in Santa Fe a little longer? Or come back after your trip to Wyoming?"

Meisner considered the question. He reached for his bag, hoisted it to one shoulder, and said, "Ja. I come back. You are only one who was interested in me. Maybe they think I am beggar or something. No one asked to see my paintings. You must make an appointment, they say."

Keith and Sonya glanced knowingly at each other; one of the charming aspects of the Twin Angels, and a few other galleries on Canyon Road, was their total lack of affectation and, in the case of the Twin Angels, a manifestation of Keith's down-to-earth personality.

"Can you come back next week?" he asked the painter.

Meisner was all smiles. "I will be here." He bent slightly, kissed Sonya's hand, hoisted his rucksack, and left.

Keith watched until he was out of sight, turned to Sonya, and shook his head in amazement. "I cannot believe this day. Now, wait'll I tell you about Marta."

CHAPTER TWENTY-THREE

Next In Line

AN IMMENSE BANK OF CLOUDS hung menacingly on the horizon all afternoon. Canyon Road had taken on a dull gray pallor, and by four o'clock the wind blew through the street, swirling leaves up and around the adobe buildings, collecting in the alleys and doorways, announcing a major storm was about to hit.

Within minutes, the sky exploded and dumped a torrent of water onto the streets and roadways, pelting the sidewalks, unlucky pedestrians, and anything else that was exposed to the elements.

Keith had an appointment with Father Dominick but wanted to wait at least until it let up before venturing out. With all his eagerness to see Martin's work, he was still hesitating to speak to Moira about it, in the event the young man, for whatever reason, didn't want to quit the Kiva to become a full-time painter: He felt an odd allegiance to Go-Go and respected the young man's reticence. But he couldn't resist talking to Téja. When he did, she started to cry.

"I am so happy, Mr. Keith, that you will see his work. I

know it is good. I know you will think it is, too. He is so shy," she told him, "and so afraid. . .but he loves the painting more than anything else."

"You know I'll do everything I can to help him, Téja."

He didn't mention the coincidental connection between him, Moira, and Martin—it didn't seem necessary.

THE RAIN STOPPED AS ABRUPTLY as it had started. Bursts of sunshine cut through the clouds like movie premier searchlights, drying the sidewalks within minutes; the pools of water, sucked down into the sewer drains, all but vanished.

Keith's pace quickened as he approached Saint Francis' Parish House. He bounded up the entry steps, scurried across the courtyard to the side entrance, and entered the office. A white-haired woman in a long-sleeve lace-collared dress, with a thin chain and minute gold cross hanging from her neck, looked up from the small reception desk.

"Good afternoon. You must be Mr. Wheeler?"

"Yes, ma'am, I am. Is Father Dominick in?"

Although the little building was detached from the basilica by a good twenty yards, he was feeling suddenly reverential and speaking to her in a voice he reserved for churches, libraries, and funeral parlors.

She seemed to levitate to her feet, a wisp of a woman, all pale pink skin and frail spindly limbs. She was wearing what his mother used to call "sensible shoes" and spoke just above a whisper. "He is expecting you. Please follow me."

She took off with a surprisingly spry step, forcing him to keep up.

"Excuse me, Father," she said at the doorway to the diminutive adobe-walled office. "Mr. Wheeler is here."

The priest pushed his padded armchair back and waved a greeting.

"Welcome, my son. How good of you to come. I am delighted by your interest in young Gomez. You won't be disappointed, I assure you. Please have a seat."

He motioned toward a straight ladder-back bench opposite his desk.

"I'm afraid our furnishings are not very comfortable, but then they're as good for the posture as they are for the soul." He chuckled, probably having made the comment to everyone who visited. Keith sat down and leaned back, immediately feeling the slats begin to press into his flesh. He slid forward as imperceptibly as possible and cleared his throat.

"I'm very excited to see more of Mr. Gomez's work. The two pieces Doña Marta showed me are exceptional."

The priest leaned toward him in a conspiratorial manner. As he did, the cross hanging from his neck swung back and forth, tapping against the desk. On the wall above Keith's head hung two photos, one of the pope and the other of the archbishop, and, above them, a copy of a Renaissance painting of St. Francis. On the wall behind Father Dominick, a large polychrome crucifix was unmistakably 17th century.

On the desk stood a very small replica of the statue of Jean Baptiste Lamy, the first Bishop of Santa Fe, modeled after the full-size version in front of the cathedral.

"I am excited for you to see them as well," said the priest. "I do not claim to be an expert on art, such as you, but I have always believed the young man had talent. When Doña Marta bought two of them on the spot, I knew he must be extraordinary."

Keith tugged gently at his earlobe, listening and nodding, and when the clergyman finished, said, "I assume then that he's agreed to show me the work. Has he discussed it with anyone else?" He was hoping he hadn't, and unsure how Moira would react when she discovered he hadn't said anything to her. "Are you aware that his aunt is my housekeeper?"

A smile crossed the other's lips. "Yes, Martin told me that after we spoke about you. It's a miracle, really, don't you think? How this has all come together right under our noses. . . just when it was needed the most."

Keith wondered if the priest knew about Paolo, or that he himself and Moira were a couple, or whether it even mattered. "I suppose it *is* a miracle of sorts. What do you mean by 'needed the most'?"

"Martin finds himself at a crucial point in his life. He believes he must give up painting to support his family, or, if he is good enough to paint professionally, quit his job. And so, he prayed for guidance. . . ."

Father Dominick closed his eyes and continued, "And the Lord intervened by introducing Marta Rodriguéz y Encantada and you, Mr. Keith Wheeler, of the Twin Angels Gallery." He opened his eyes. "Isn't that something?"

Keith wondered if the priest truly believed it was a miracle.

"Perhaps you're right, Father. Perhaps it is divine intervention."

He studied the priest's face for a few seconds and then looked at his hands, wondering how many signs of the cross Father Dominick had made with them over the years. It was a curious thought. "When may I see the work?" he finally asked.

"He agreed to let you visit his studio at your convenience. He said he would ask for the time off at work."

"Shall I go by myself, or will you be joining me?"

"I discussed this with Martin, and he is perfectly agreeable with you coming alone. He said you know the way because you have taken Téja home from time to time."

Keith sat pondering the irony, the coincidence, or whether, maybe, it really was some kind of miracle. "I'll take it from here if that's okay with you, then, Father. I can stop in at the Kiva this afternoon and talk to him. "

"That would be wonderful. Thank you for your help. *Vaya con dios*, my son. And do let me know the outcome."

"Of course I will."

KEITH HASTENED BACK TO THE GALLERY, stopped abruptly at the entrance, turned around and crossed the street, and went into the Kiva. Not yet open for dinner, the place was empty.

He went into the kitchen, where the commotion, clatter, and a cacophony of sound accosted him as soon as he stepped onto the rubber matted floor. Steam rose from stainless steel counters; the chef was sampling a pumpkin squash soup that gave off the aroma of sweet basil, rosemary, and jicama mingled with the faint smell of toasted pine nuts.

He knocked at the door frame to Moira's minuscule office.

"Hi, honey, I'm home!"

She flinched in surprise and swiveled around to look at him. "Heya. What are you doing here?"

"Hi. You got a minute?"

She glanced at the plain wall clock and back at him. "Sure."

There was no place to sit, so he moved closer and shut the door.

"Uh-oh. What's up?" she asked.

He kissed her on the top of her head. "You remember telling me you had somebody here that was a painter, but you weren't sure about his work?"

She put her pen down and sat back. "Uh-huh. What about it?"

"Moira, I was contacted by Marta Rodríguez a few days ago and she asked me to look at an artist's work. . .who turned out to be Martin."

"*My* Martin?"

"Yes." He chuckled at the inference. "*Your* Martin."

She registered total surprise. "Really? You're kidding. . . I mean, how did that happen?"

"Okay, so he *is* the one you were talking about, but didn't know if he was any good, right?"

"Right, but I still don't know."

"That's the thing. Marta came to me because she'd seen his work."

"Wait a minute. How did *that* happen?"

He pushed some paperwork aside and sat on the edge of her desk. "It seems Martin has been painting for a long time, and Father Dominick—"

"You mean from Saint Francis? How'd he know about it?"

"Hang on."

"Sorry, go ahead."

"Father Dominick sponsored Martin when he was in the after-school art program and helped him get a scholarship to the Art Institute, but the kid had to quit before graduating."

"I didn't know anything about that."

"I know," Keith reassured her. "All this time he continued to paint, but he never showed his work to anyone."

"Go on."

"Not too long ago—oh, by the way, Martin's aunt is my housekeeper, Téja."

"Oh. This is getting even better."

"Yeah, and she never said anything to me about him being a painter, can you believe that? Anyway, Father Dominick said that, one day, Martin came to him and told him he was thinking of giving up painting because it conflicted with his job."

"Wait a minute! How long ago was that?"

"I'm not sure. Why?"

"Martin came in late one day covered with paint, but he wouldn't tell me what was going on."

"Could've been around the same time. Anyway, what happened is, Father Dominick tells Martin he'll help him, so he calls Doña Marta and asks her to look at the art." Keith paused for effect. "Now, get this—*she* goes absolutely gaga over his stuff, buys two paintings on the spot and then calls to tell *me* about it and brings the work to the gallery."

"And?"

"And it's *fabulous!* I'm going to see the rest of it—"

"You mean there's more?"

"Moira, the kid has a studio full of work. Don't you see? If he's as good as Marta and I think, he'll not only replace Rinaldi at the Twin Angels, he might even be better."

"Wow! So when are you going to see it?"

"I hope to go Monday, but I wanted you to know about this before I did anything. I mean, if he's that good, he needs to paint full time. That'll mean—"

"Quitting here."

"Right."

"Y'know, I'd hate to lose him, but he is such a sweet young man and deserves a break. I'd be thrilled for him."

Keith's face lit up. "There wasn't a doubt in my mind that you'd feel that way—another reason I love you."

A tiny smile started in the corner of her mouth and slowly worked its way into a grin. "Well, I love you too, Mister Secret Keeper." She stood up and kissed him. "Did you speak to Martin yet?"

"No, I wanted to let you know and make sure you were okay with it."

"I'm more than okay with it. I'm ecstatic for both of you. Do you want me to say anything to him?"

"Let me see the work first. If it's that good, then I'll tell him you're okay with the whole thing."

"Fine with me," she assured him. "*it*'s your call."

"I asked Cydney to hostess next Saturday," she said, "so we can have our long overdue picnic with Deirdre."

"That's *great!* Deirdre is so excited about seeing you again."

Moira grinned, then looked at her desk. "I have to get back

to work—it's almost time for me to be out front."

"I'll talk to you later."

On his way out, Keith stopped to talk to Martin. "Martin, got a sec?"

"Y-Yes." The young man stopped folding napkins.

"Do you remember me? I'm Keith Wheeler, from the Twin Angels gallery. Your aunt is my housekeeper. I have seen some of your art work. Doña Marta showed two paintings to me, and I'm very impressed. Father Dominick told me I can come to visit your studio. Is Monday okay?"

He stammered, "Y-yes," but was clearly uncomfortable and seemed unsure of what to say.

Keith placated him. "It's all right. The work I have seen so far is *incredibly* good."

He remained a blank canvas to Keith. It was as if the young man didn't quite comprehend what was happening, and he very probably didn't.

Keith pulled a chair away from the table and sat down. "Martin, please, sit down for a minute. I am sure that Moira would be very happy for you."

Martin, still looked confused and suddenly stammered, "I d-don't know if I can make enough m-*money* from painting, Señor Wheeler."

Keith leaned in and looked into the artist's eyes. "Let me say something to you that I have a feeling you can understand more than most people. Perhaps you will not make a great deal of money, but you are rich in other ways. An artist, Martin, takes joy in the process of creation, in the pursuit of an idea and bringing it to fruition. You have been given a gift, and you must be grateful that you were chosen. Take the gift and cherish it for all it gives to you and those who you share it with . . . and, that said, I think the money *will* come. I have every confidence in you and your talent."

Martin shrugged, looked down at his feet, and then back at Keith. "W-when d-do you want to c-c-come?"

"I can be there at eleven. Will that be all right?"

Martin nodded several times, and, looking at Keith's chest rather than in his eyes, he held out his hand and mumbled, "Th-Thank you, Señor Wheeler."

"No, no, thank *you*, Martin. And call me Keith. I'll see you on Monday."

CHAPTER TWENTY-THREE

Destiny

DOÑA MARTA ADJUSTED CALLO'S SADDLE and led him out of the courtyard. "Douglas, we'll be out for an hour or so."

"Viento will be jealous, Doña Marta."

"I'm sure, but I'll take him next time."

"Have a good ride. I'll give the Andalucían a flake or two while you are gone."

"Thank you, Douglas—I'm sure some fresh hay will make him forget I didn't take him out today."

He patted the horse's flank and stepped back while Marta gracefully mounted the Morgan and walked him outside the gate, slowly leading him toward the ridge. The air was tinged with autumn. Leaves crunched like gravel under the horse's hooves. Marta zipped her fleece vest a little higher and then gently kicked Callo's flanks to trot.

When they came to an arroyo, she gradually eased up on the reins and nudged the horse with her heel. He went obligingly into a gallop and moved swiftly across the open field toward the trees ringing the far end of the property. She pressed her knee into his flank and headed toward the ridge.

A contented smile lit Marta's face. The brisk wind blowing through her hair filled her senses. A few minutes into the gallop, she guided the horse up the trail, climbing toward the crest of the hill overlooking Santa Fe and the Rodríguez-Encantada hacienda. From the time she learned to ride as a spirited, strong-willed six-year-old, it had been her favorite vista in all of New Mexico.

Owning the land that had been in her family for more than a hundred and fifty years gave her a sense of pride, security, and comfort.

With no immediate family to leave it to, she thought she might sell it one day; but each time she looked out over the landscape from that very spot, she knew she could never do that.

Dismounting, she walked Callo as she led him loosely by the reins and stopped at a stream to let him drink. She took several deep, lung-filling breaths, sat on the overlook taking in the hundred-mile view, tilted her head back, closed her eyes, and bathed in the luxurious warmth of the morning sun.

The horse nudged her with his head and brought her back to the present. She smiled, hooked her arm around his massive neck, rose to her feet, patted him, and remounted. "What's wrong?" she asked. "Feeling neglected?" She laughed at the thought and started back.

A FEW DAYS AFTER HE SCHEDULED a visit to Martin, Keith entered the artist's studio and was immediately struck by the number of paintings spread around. They were dazzling, and his eyes darted from one to another, stopping momentarily to study one or two and then move on, viewing each a second time before moving closer to examine them. Martin offered no comment but watched as Keith bent down, then stood up, without uttering a word. It was almost unbearable to him not knowing what would happen if Keith didn't like the work.

Finally, Keith took hold of a paint-splattered chair and sat down. He ran a hand through his hair and peered at him, then started to laugh happily. "Martin. . .these are fantastic!"

Go-Go stared at him in disbelief, his round, cherubic face damp with sweat, his expression a mixture of fear and excitement.

"I mean it. I haven't seen work like this in years, and never such a diverse range from one artist. . .ever. You have a great gift, and I'd like very much to represent you."

Martin stammered, swallowed once, and vigorously nodded. "Yes, yes. . .I would. I mean y-yes, you can."

Keith rose and rested a hand on Martin's shoulder. "You know what this means, right?"

It was apparent that the artist wasn't quite sure.

"It means—" Keith took a breath— "it means you probably won't have to work at the Kiva anymore. It means that you will be able to paint all the time. It means you will be able to—"

Martin tried hard to hold back the tears, but they came all the same. He swiped at one eye with his finger and then brushed the hair back off of his forehead.

"I have to t-talk to Aunt Téja and M-Moira."

"Yes, of course, I understand."

He instinctively hugged Keith and then nodded several

times, not wanting him to leave, afraid he might change his mind.

"Martin, take as much time as you need to get things in order. When you are ready, stop by the gallery and we can talk about arrangements, a contract, nothing complicated. I think you have enough work here to stage an opening within a couple of months. . .if you are willing."

"Yes. I am w-willing. I am willing."

ON HIS WAY BACK TO TOWN, Keith called Moira. "Hey!"

"Hey, yourself. How'd it go?"

"Fantastic! Moira, the kid is sensational. I mean it!"

"Really? Wow, who'd've known?"

"I'm astounded. He's so talented and has such an amazing range of work. I—I can't believe it. And he has no idea how good he is. I mean, he's humble, almost embarrassed by it."

"I can hear the excitement in your voice. That's wonderful, for Martin. . .and for you."

Still reeling from what he had seen, Keith's enthusiasm grew. "This is just so amazing. I have an idea Martin will be very successful and have more money than he ever dreamed possible."

"Oh, Keith, that is marvelous. What next?"

"Well, I think you better start looking for a new waiter."

She laughed. "How much time do I have?"

"It all depends on him—when, and if in fact, he can make the move."

"Why? Do you think he won't?"

"I don't know. He seems scared, confused, but I'll do everything I can to help him and make it easier. I plan to buy a couple of his pieces for myself, and that should give him a head start."

"Well, maybe I will, too."

"That would be terrific. Let's talk about it tomorrow, okay?"

"Yes, but only a little. I want us to spend tomorrow with Deirdre and not take time away from her."

DEIRDRE GOT OUT OF BED, washed up, and was already dressed when Keith came in to wake her.

"Hi, honey. Look at you all dressed! Did you get washed, too?"

"Yes, Daddy."

She had put on a pair of faded blue jeans with butterfly patches on the back pockets, pink sneakers with white trim, and a long-sleeved T-shirt. Her hair was clipped to the side with one pink and one white plastic barrette.

"You look very pretty, sweetie. You must be excited about today."

"Yes. Is Moy-rah, excited?"

"I bet she is. I know she's been looking forward to it."

She gave him a hug. "I'm bringing my backpack…so I can carry stuff."

"What do you plan to carry?"

"My water bottle, my book, my—"

"What book?"

"I'm bringing a book to read so you and Moy-rah can have alone time. You know, Dad, I'm six. You don't have to entertain me."

He couldn't help laugh at her precociousness, scooped her up in his arms, and kissed her. "How did I get so lucky?"

She giggled and said, "Put me down. We have to have breakfast and make the sandwiches."

"Oh, right. What are we going to make?"

"Um-mm. . . ." She put a finger to her lips.

He waited as she gave the idea some serious consideration, and then her eyes widened.

"I know," she said excitedly. "We can make grill cheese sandwiches!"

"Well," he said cautiously, "we could. But they'd be pretty soggy by the time we ate them, don't you think?"

"Oh, I know, I know! How about turkey? That won't get yukky."

"Well, that might work. Is that what you want?"

"Uh-huh. Do you think she'll eat that?"

He was thrilled that she'd asked. "Absolutely! You make great sandwiches."

She took his hand and headed into the kitchen, where he set her down on the granite counter top, gathered the ingredients, and placed them next to her.

"Here y'go, sweetums. You make the sandwiches, and I'll make breakfast. Fruit Loops okay?"

ACROSS TOWN, MOIRA SAT UP, stretched, yawned, and glanced at the clock. It was so rare she got to sleep late, if seven-thirty qualified as late. Bruleé was curled up on the pillow next to her and woke at her stirring. The cat straightened her tiny limbs, shuddered once, arched her back, and started kneading the covers with her front paws.

Moira ran her hand down the animal's length and along its tail, and then she flicked the fur from her fingers. She instinctively pulled her other fingers through her own hair, trying to untangle the twisted strands.

She yawned again and flung back the covers, causing the cat to jump off with a thump and scurry out of the room. Swinging her bare legs over the side, she wiggled her toes, stepped barefoot onto the floor, shuffled into the bathroom, and took a shower.

When she was finished, she wrapped herself in a terry robe and tied a towel around her wet hair.

She had plain yogurt and a mug of black coffee for breakfast, picked through the accumulated mail, separating the bills from the advertising flyers, perused the newspaper, and then called Keith.

"G'mornin', handsome. We still on for today?"

"Hi. Good morning to you. Yes, absolutely. I'm surprised Deirdre isn't sitting in the car already, she's so excited."

"Are you still thinking noontime?" she asked.

"Yeah, that okay?"

"Uh-huh, I'll look for you then."

HE AND DEIRDRE DROVE to the market and bought some additional things to eat. "Just in case we're still hungry after your delicious sandwiches, honey," he explained.

When they got to Moira's house, Deirdre scrambled over the front seat and planted herself in the back. "Now Moy-rah can sit next to you, Dad."

"That's really nice. Thank you."

Moira appeared in jeans, a long-sleeved pullover, a black sweater tied around her neck, and a pony tail pulled through the back of a Dodgers baseball cap. She slid into the car, kissed Keith, and then reached back to Deirdre. "Hi, everyone! How are you, Deirdre?"

"I'm fine, thank you."

"It's a beautiful day, isn't it? Why don't we go on a picnic?"

Deirdre giggled. "That's where we're *going*, silly!"

On the drive north to Ghost Ranch, Deirdre chattered like a monkey, glancing back and forth from Moira to Keith, smiling the whole time.

When they got there and parked the car, she scrambled out, threw her arms around Moira, and held on for a long time.

Moira returned the hug, looking at Keith, surprised but happy with the show of affection. He winked and nodded.

"Moy-rah, will you be my mommy?"

Caught off guard, she didn't know what to say, and Deirdre turned toward Keith. "Daddy?"

He looked at Moira and gave her a tiny smile. "Deirdre, honey, that's not the kind of question to ask someone."

Moira crouched so she was eye level with the child and took hold of her tiny hands. She studied the little fingers and then touched Deirdre's cheek.

"You know, Deirdre, that is something your daddy and I haven't talked about yet, so I can't answer you. But I do like you a whole lot, and we will always be friends. I can never be your mommy, but I *could* be your step-mommy."

Deirdre thought about it for a few seconds, put her arms around Moira's neck, stepped back, and looked at her. "Step-mommies are mean. You're not. You're nice."

"Well, honey, sometimes step-mommies are mean in fairy tales, but usually not in real life."

The child pondered that for a couple of seconds, kissed Moira on the cheek, and cheerfully said, "Okay." Then she bounded off as if the conversation hadn't taken place.

Keith put the food into a backpack, turned slowly toward Moira, took her hand and said, "Y'know, we might want to talk about that sometime."

"How about now?"

"Okay. Moira, will you marry me?"

Her eyes filled with tears, and she put her arms around him, pressed her face to his chest, and whispered in his ear, "Yes, Yes! Yes!"

They held each other's gaze for a moment and went off in pursuit of Deirdre, who by then was laughing happily in the distance.

The little girl stopped, turned to see if they were following, put her hands on her hips, and called to them. "Come on, you guys, catch up."

CHAPTER TWENTY-FOUR

Conclusion

WITH ALL THE PAINTINGS MARTIN had stock-piled, it didn't take long to pull a show together. In a bit of irony, the reception originally planned for Paolo was opportunely rescheduled for Martin's debut. Advertisements were placed in regional newspapers and in national art magazines touting the introduction of "Paintings by Martin Gomez."

"Go-Go" had no frame of reference for what was happening or how his life had already changed, and he more than once expressed ambivalence about leaving his job at the Kiva. Moira tried to reassure him that he *was* ready, and that the decision was the right one.

"But how c-can you be s-sure?" he asked her.

"Martin, trust Keith. He knows exactly what he is doing. You know how much Doña Marta likes your art, and I also think it's beautiful. Keith wouldn't represent you if he didn't think you had the talent and ability to be a success."

In an ironic twist, Martin's gallery reception would be the first art opening he ever attended. His nervousness was palpable; he stammered more than usual and fidgeted when talking to Keith, but with encouragement and compassion, he eventually relaxed enough to feel the joy of the moment. Not surprisingly, in the time leading up to the event, he managed to take refuge from the outside world and from his own mind games by painting. Though the work for the show had long since been selected, he lost himself to his muse when he was moving his paint-laden brush around a canvas. It was in his studio that he felt safe, where nothing redirected his attention, where doubt was a distant demon.

A LITTLE BEFORE THE RECEPTION BEGAN, the sun melded into the horizon and transformed the sky into a sapphire blanket spreading blue shadows over Canyon Road.

A few invited guests arrived earlier than the seven P.M. opening and hung around on the sidewalk in front of the gallery, chattering about the Twin Angels' "new find." By the time the doors were officially open, a dozen people were ready to eagerly file in.

Martin wore a black sport jacket over a pink shirt purchased just for the occasion, and although he looked positively bewildered, he managed to smile and shake hands when Keith introduced him as the single most exciting emerging artist he ever encountered.

Marta Rodríguez y Encantada arrived at seven-thirty, with Father Dominick as her escort. They went directly to where Martin was standing, waited a moment to catch his attention, and then shook his hand.

"Martin," offered Father Dominick, "I am so proud of you!

We all are."

Martin smiled shyly and replied, "*Gracias, Padre.* I am h-happy you are here."

Marta took a step closer and said, "Congratulations, young man. I am delighted for you and expect tonight to be a great success. The Santa Fe art community is fortunate to call you a native son."

"Thank you, Doña Marta. I would not be here if you did not help me."

Although he had rehearsed the words several times throughout the day, it was the first time he had delivered them without a stutter, but neither he, Marta, nor the priest took notice.

The exhibit was stunning in its completeness. Keith had chosen wisely, and every painting suggested the artist was accomplished and unique. Four paintings, priced between $2,500 and $3,500, were sold within the first hour. People entered the gallery at different times, but few left, staying instead to meet Martin and revisit a particular work they admired or contemplated buying. There was animated chatter in the air, champagne and canapés consumed, greetings heard from across the room, and praise for both Keith and Martin occurred at regular intervals.

At one point, Sonya had to limit entry to one or two at a time until the crowd thinned out.

At another, Keith glanced at the doorway and caught a glimpse of a man across the street in the shadows of Canyon Road, the glow of his cigarette growing brighter as he puffed on it. Not until he recognized the red sports car parked adjacent to the gallery did he realize it was Paolo Rinaldi.

Moira slid her hand into Keith's and followed his gaze. She too recognized the Alpha Romeo and whispered, "No invitation, I guess?"

Keith squeezed her hand once and sarcastically replied, "Must've gotten lost in the mail. I can't imagine what happened. I sent it the same time as Hollingsworth's."

The reception was slated to end at nine P.M., but several people lingered, wanting to talk with Martin, who by then was dazed, but elated. Eight of the paintings had been sold, which, with a fifty-percent commission going to the gallery, netted $12,000 for Martin, marking his debut a mini-triumph as well as a brilliant introduction to the art world.

If anyone was smiling more that night than he or Keith, it was his Aunt Téja and his three siblings.

ABOUT THE AUTHOR

Stew Mosberg retired from a successful career in design to write full-time and is the author of two books on design. He published *The Cultural Times*, a monthly arts magazine, was the Colorado correspondent for *Art Talk Magazine*, and was a staff writer for *Arts Perspective* magazine. He taught at the School of Visual Arts and Parsons School of Design in New York City. His writing has appeared in publications nationally and internationally. Stew currently resides in Southwest Colorado, just a few hours' drive from Santa Fe. *In the Shadows of Canyon Road* is his first full-length novel.